Murder in Ashmere

A Cozy Mystery

Estelle Hartley

First Edition

Farbellum Press

www.farbellum.com

Cover design by Farbellum Press

ISBN: [978-1-7641306-7-7] Paperback

Contents

Chapter 1: Homecoming

The engine of the Ford Focus gave its familiar grumble as Isla coaxed it around the final bend, the transmission hiccupping like it couldn't decide which gear to commit to.

"Just get me there, bud," she muttered, tightening her grip on the steering wheel.

The Hudson Valley rolled out around her, green hills and sleepy towns that looked nothing like the pulsing sidewalks of Brooklyn she'd just left behind. The strange thing was, she wasn't even that far from the city. An hour and change, if you didn't hit traffic. Close enough to smell ambition in the air, far enough that no one cared about your job title.

In the back seat, a mix of hastily packed bags rattled with every bump. Clothes half-folded, a plant tipping sideways, and a beat-up notebook that had followed her through three apartments and two heartbreaks. No photos in frames, not anymore. That had been boxed and left behind, like most things she didn't want to think too hard about.

The fuel light pinged. Again.

Isla sighed. "Of course you're hungry."

She flicked down the sun visor to check her reflection. The wind from the open window had turned her hair into a soft kind of chaos, strands curling at their own free will. A faded hoodie hung off one shoulder, and her jeans, once black, had seen better dye jobs. A tattoo peeked out from under her sleeve, inked across her left wrist like a quiet dare she hadn't explained to anyone in years.

When she finally pulled into the driveway, the Focus made one last mechanical protest before giving up and cutting out completely.

She exhaled. *"Good car,"* she said, giving the dash a soft pat.

The cottage sat at the end of the street, its shutters slightly crooked, its porch sagging like a tired sigh. It had looked *quaint* in the online listing, a word that could mean "charming" or "cheap," depending on who was writing it. Isla had needed affordable, and this place hadn't been lived in for a while. She was told it came furnished, which, at this point in her life, meant one less thing to worry about.

She grabbed her key from her bag, marched up the steps, and unlocked the front door. The hinges shrieked as it swung open.

Dust greeted her like an old friend. It billowed into the sunlight, catching in the air like glitter if glitter was made of sneeze.

She coughed, waving a faded pizza menu she'd grabbed off the entry table.

Then: a sound.

A low, unmistakable hiss.

Isla turned just in time to see it: a raccoon perched smugly on the side table; eyes narrowed like it had been waiting for her.

"Oh, hell no," she blurted.

The raccoon responded with a sharper hiss, then bolted. It darted past her legs and vanished through the still-open front door, trailing dust and indignation behind it.

Isla stood in the silence that followed, hands on her knees, catching her breath.

"Home sweet home."

Isla popped the hatch of her car, reaching in to grab a duffel bag that had half-unzipped itself during the drive. A sock dangled from the side like a white flag. She sighed, pushed her hair back into its loose bun, and slung the bag over her shoulder. The breeze off the river carried the scent of pine, late-summer grass, and maybe honeysuckle; or maybe just nostalgia trying to smell nice.

Just as she shut the trunk..

"Well, you're not the mailman."

Isla turned. A pair of eyes peered through a gap in the hedge, beneath the brim of an oversized sun hat that looked like it had once attended a 1950s gardening competition and refused to leave.

"I'm Binnie," the woman announced, stepping out with gloved hands and pruning shears that had seen more gossip than garden work. "Binnie Quimby. You're new."

"Uh, hi. Isla. Isla Winters. I just moved here. Well, renting."

"You don't look like you garden."

"Sorry?"

"Those shoes." Binnie squinted. "Not practical. And that top… is it inside out, or just… confused?"

Isla looked down. It might've been both.

"I, umm maybe."

"No matter. You're young. You can afford to be chaotic." Binnie leaned on her shears. "What brings you back? Divorce? Scandal? Witness protection?"

Isla opened her mouth.

"Oh, never mind," Binnie waved it off. "I'll guess by Tuesday."

A pause.

"I'm glad someone's in that place again," Binnie continued. "The man before you used to feed his cat six times a day. Six! I told him, you're not fattening it for winter. He said 'she's just hungry.' I said, *she's a liar.* That cat was manipulating him."

Just then, as if summoned, a plump tabby waddled across the gravel path between them, tail high and face smug with satisfaction. It paused to sit in a patch of sunlight and licked its paw like it had just conquered Rome.

Binnie stared at it. Slowly, solemnly, she gave a tiny shake of her head; a quiet gesture of deep disapproval, as if the cat had once broken her heart and never apologized.

"She knows what she did," Binnie whispered.

Then she turned back to Isla, lowering her voice with sudden seriousness. "You know… stay around for a bit, and I'll tell you some *real* stories, Isla."

She winked.

And then, like a breeze passing through hedgerows, she disappeared.

Isla stood there, half a grocery bag in hand, as the cat rolled onto its side with a satisfied grunt.

"Right," she muttered, "we're off to a completely normal start."

The screen door creaked shut behind her with a wheeze like it hadn't had company in years. Isla stood in the center of the small living room, her hands on her hips, taking it all in.

The listing had said "fully furnished." Technically true, she supposed, in the same way a child's drawing is "technically a portrait."

There was a three-seater couch pushed against the far wall, its cushions slumped like they'd survived something traumatic. A single rocking chair sat on the front verandah, gently moving with the wind, though Isla couldn't tell if it was haunted or just optimistic.

In the adjoining kitchen, she found a rickety metal table from the fifties and two mismatched chairs with peeling vinyl seats. On the countertop sat one lonely mug, slightly chipped, with the words *Gone Fishin'* curling in faded red letters. She picked it up, turned it over. Dry. Dusty. Probably safe.

The fridge, a beige block of stubbornness, hummed to life only after she slapped the side of it. "Just like my car," she muttered.

Dust lay thick across the floorboards, undisturbed except where her boots had left new patterns. The air smelled of cedar, old paper, and the kind of silence that builds up when no one's lived in a place for too long. Isla was half concerned, half curious about what else might be nesting in the premise.

She dropped her duffel beside the couch, collapsing onto it with a sigh. Springs groaned. Isla leaned her head back and stared at the cracked ceiling like it owed her something.

Her reflection caught faintly in the window's twilight glass, wild brunette waves escaping her loose bun, olive-toned skin flushed from the drive, dark jeans smudged with lint and life. Her hoodie was oversized, and the ink of her faded wrist tattoo peeked out near the sleeve: a tiny line drawing of a mountain, etched during a reckless Brooklyn night years ago. The only thing tidy about her was her striking green eyes: sharp, alert, like they were always trying to solve something the rest of her hadn't caught up to yet.

"Well," she said to no one, raising the chipped mug, "to new beginnings, however dusty."

She pushed off the couch, set the mug on the counter, and grabbed a broom from the corner like it was an old friend. Her phone slid from her pocket, clattering to the counter. A few taps, and music filled the little house; one of her old playlists, part indie rock, part nostalgia, all hers.

As the first beat kicked in, Isla began to sweep. Dust spun into the air like ghosts let loose. She danced her way around furniture, occasionally singing under her breath, boots scuffing the floor in rhythm.

Outside, the sun dipped behind the trees. Light streamed through the dusty windows in golden shafts, catching particles in flight.

Inside, a girl in torn jeans and too many layers swept away someone else's past, and maybe a little of her own.

Chapter 2: Morning

Isla woke tangled in a thin blanket, limbs half draped off the faded three-seater. Her feet were bare and cold against the wooden floorboards, and her sleep shirt had twisted uncomfortably in the night, clinging to her side. She groaned, rubbing a hand over her face.

Sunlight poured in through the crooked blinds. Way too much of it, too early.

She sat up slowly, hair wild and stuck to one side of her face. Her jeans hung from the front door's knob, like they'd tried to escape in the middle of the night and failed. She pulled them on without thinking, hopping slightly as she jammed her foot through a wayward belt loop.

Padding into the kitchen, she rifled through her one small shopping bag of essentials and grabbed an instant coffee sachet. With one eye still closed against the light, she gave the "Gone Fishin'" mug a half-hearted wipe on her sleep shirt and filled it with water after waiting impatiently for the kettle to boil.

No creamer. No milk. Isla had found a chopstick though to double as a stirrer.

She stepped out onto the front porch with the steaming mug, settling into the old rocking chair like someone twice her age. She stared ahead at the quiet street. There was one car parked a few houses down, a bird darting between the trees, the world already moving without her.

Isla took a sip. Burned her tongue. Sighed.

She was not a morning person. Never had been.

The porch creaked softly beneath her bare feet as Isla leaned back in the old rocking chair, sipping burnt instant coffee and trying to wake up without participating in the day just yet.

But the universe, or more specifically, Ashmere, had other plans.

"Well, look who's up with the sun!"

Isla nearly spilled her coffee.

As if out of nowhere, with the energy of a mountain lion, Binnie Quimby pounced around the hedge, eyes locked onto her target like a heat-seeking missile. Isla could practically hear a dramatic wildlife documentary narrator in her head: *"There. Just beyond the porch steps. The morning's unsuspecting prey…"*

There was no escape. The predator had found her.

Binnie stepped fully onto the porch without hesitation, not so much as a pause at the boundary between private and public space. She adjusted her enormous sun hat, hands on hips like she was about to appraise the entire layout of Isla's soul.

"You sleep all right?" she asked. "I heard something rustling in the bins last night it sounded like raccoons again. Nasty little things. Have you seen one?"

Isla took another sip of her coffee, stalling.

"Yeah," she said dryly. "I'm actually a raccoon breeder. Moved here to expand the operation."

Binnie blinked. For half a second, Isla thought she might believe it.

Then Binnie let out a loud, delighted "HA!" and clapped once, as if Isla had just performed a trick.

"Oh, you're going to fit in just fine," she said, nodding sagely. "We don't get enough sarcasm in Ashmere. Most people just say 'bless your heart' and talk behind your back."

She settled into the second chair on the porch, uninvited but perfectly at home.

She settled into the second chair on the porch, uninvited but perfectly at home.

"Have you been to Riverbend Books?" Binnie asked suddenly, her eyes narrowing like she was checking if Isla had passed some unspoken test. "Oh, you should go. They don't get that many sales these days; everyone's always 'Amazoning' or whatever it's called but the lady that owns it…" she leaned forward as if revealing a myth, "…she's a strange one. I think a book or two might be written about her one day."

Before Isla could respond, Binnie was already pushing herself up from the chair with surprising agility for someone her age, as if her sole task of spreading this precise piece of information had now been accomplished.

"Well, I should water the tomatoes before they revolt," she said, tipping her hat. "You know where to find me if you need sugar or scandal."

Then she was gone, slipping back behind the hedge like a reverse apparition, leaving only the scent of sunblock and gardenias behind.

Isla sat there for a moment longer, blinking at the now-empty chair beside her.

"That woman's powered by gossip and Gatorade," she muttered, taking another sip of gritty instant coffee.

The Ford Focus sputtered awake like it had been woken from a bad dream.

Isla winced at the groan from the engine. "You and me both, bud," she muttered, giving the dashboard a light thump, her version of encouragement. The gas needle hovered just above empty, as if too tired to commit to honesty.

She backed out of the gravel drive, the tires crunching softly beneath her, and turned onto the main road that curved toward town.

Ashmere unrolled around her like an old photograph; faded at the edges, but still familiar.

The trees arched overhead, sun slanting through their leaves like light filtering through stained glass. The sidewalk cracked in all the same places it had when she was a teenager walking home from school, backpack lopsided and headphones always in.

She passed the Ashmere Fire Station first; squat, red-bricked, with its single bay door propped open like it had nothing to hide. A pair of folding chairs sat just outside in the sun, one of them occupied by a man in uniform cradling a Styrofoam cup and nodding off like it was part of his job description. A hand-painted sign above the entrance still read *Home of the Ashmere Fire Hawks*, even though no one had worn that nickname seriously since the '90s.

The general store still had the World War II posters in the window. Amos Reeve's truck sat out front, exactly where it had always been parked: half in the lines, half daring someone to complain.

A little farther down, she caught sight of Riverbend Books. It was tucked between a closed bakery and a hair salon with a crooked "Walk-Ins Welcome" sign. The bookstore's display window held a lopsided pyramid of cozy mystery paperbacks, a hand-painted sign reading "You Belong Here (Even If You're Just Browsing)." Isla smiled. That felt like the kind of place she might need.

A train horn sounded faintly from across the river, its echo cutting through the quiet like a memory.

She slowed at a four-way stop, no other cars in sight, and let the moment stretch. The breeze nudged the hanging baskets on the lampposts, purple petunias swinging like sleepy parade dancers.

Ashmere was still Ashmere. A little more chipped around the edges, maybe. A little more hollowed out. But it was here. Still standing. Still itself.

And maybe, just maybe, that was enough for now.

She pulled into an empty spot outside the diner and killed the engine. The Focus coughed once as if a final protest, then went still.

Isla exhaled and rested her hands on the wheel.

"Well," she said softly, "let's see if the town remembers me.

The bell over the door gave a cheerful jingle, the kind that pretended time hadn't passed; that this was still a world of newspaper crossword puzzles without asking.

The Ashmere Diner looked almost exactly the same as Isla remembered: red vinyl booths worn smooth at the seams, sun-bleached photos of town events lining the walls, and a dessert display case that hadn't rotated properly since Clinton was in office. The air smelled like coffee, maple syrup, and a hint of bacon that had somehow soaked into the linoleum itself.

She paused near the entrance, letting her eyes adjust to the light and the memory. Locals dotted the room: a man in a tractor cap arguing with his toast, two older women debating bingo rules with surgical precision. The town hadn't just preserved this place. It had *paused* it.

Then she saw her.

Tessa Blake sat in a booth near the window, waving a hand above her head like a flag Isla had forgotten she needed. Same quick grin, same freckled cheeks, same bright eyes under a messy ponytail that hadn't changed since high school; only now with a dash of knowing behind them.

Isla's chest tightened, then loosened. Somehow, Tessa still had that same young face like life had happened around her, not to her. Even though Isla knew the stories said otherwise. Married young. Divorced quietly. Stayed in town the whole time.

She crossed the diner, sliding into the booth across from her.

The cushion gave a tired sigh beneath her.

Tessa raised her mug. "Thought maybe you'd chickened out."

Isla smirked.

And just like that, the years between them began to crumble.

Tessa raised her mug. "You still take your coffee black? Or did the city turn you into one of those triple-foam hazelnut swirl types with oat milk and moral superiority?"

Isla let her bag slide to the booth seat beside her. "Please. I'm not that far gone. Just emotionally dehydrated."

Tessa grinned. "You always were. Even at fifteen, you were eighty inside."

Isla smiled back, brushing a few wild strands of hair behind her ear, a losing battle. The breeze had caught her on the walk in, and now a few curls clung to her cheek like determined vines. She tugged at her sleeve, smoothing it down out of instinct more than care.

"I forgot how damp this town is," she muttered. "I've been here twelve hours and already look like a before photo."

Tessa gave her a once-over, half-teasing, half-tender. "You look like you. That's the good part."

Isla raised an eyebrow. "So... slightly feral and undercaffeinated?"

"Exactly."

A moment passed, the silence comfortable, coffee warm.

Tessa leaned back against the booth. "I kept expecting you to message me. Every couple years I'd think, 'This is the time Isla reaches out.' And then... nothing."

"I kept thinking the same thing. Just... flipped." Isla shrugged, eyes on her mug. "Sometimes it's easier to stay gone than explain why you left."

Tessa tilted her head. "That deep thought come with your city rent?"

"No," Isla smirked. "That one was free with my heartbreak and a half-used MetroCard."

Tessa snorted. "Well, now you're back. Permanently?"

Isla hesitated. "Renting. That's as permanent as I get right now."

"Fair. Commitment is a slippery eel."

"Did you just call me an eel?"

"If the shoe fits."

They both laughed and Isla felt something shift. Just a click, small and quiet. Like a drawer that hadn't been opened in years sliding back into place.

"So," Isla asked, "still running that flower shop?"

"Barely. Half the town thinks carnations are a personality trait and the other half just wants cheap succulents they can't kill."

"Sounds like a dream."

"It smells like one," Tessa said. "Even when business is bad, I open the door and it hits me. It's soil and jasmine and hope. It's like... aromatherapy for disappointment."

Isla stirred her coffee with the edge of her spoon. "I used to think about that. Staying. Small life. Knowing everyone."

"You wouldn't have lasted two weeks," Tessa said, smiling. "You'd be climbing the water tower just for something to do."

"Maybe. Maybe not." Isla looked out the window, where the light was starting to shift across the diner sign. "I just wanted something quiet. Something that didn't ask for explanations."

"You'll get that here. People will judge you, but they won't ask."

"Oh good," Isla deadpanned. "Ashmere: come for the gossip, stay for the passive-aggressive pie."

They both laughed again, easier this time.

"Hey girls," came a voice from behind, "you planning to order, or just working through decades of emotional repression?"

Della Jean stood beside the booth, hand on her hip, eyebrow arched with surgical precision. Her earrings looked like miniature jellyfish today, and Isla couldn't help but admire the commitment.

"Two coffees," Tessa said, not missing a beat, "and a reset button."

Della scribbled it down like it was the day's special. "Coming right up. And Isla, you better eat something. You look like a breeze could knock you sideways."

"I'll take that as a compliment," Isla said.

"You shouldn't," Della replied, already walking off.

Tessa leaned in, voice low. "She likes you. That's her version of rolling out the red carpet."

Isla smiled, tucking her hair back again as another curl bounced loose.

Tessa took a slow sip of her coffee, watching Isla over the rim. "So where are you living? Please don't say you're crashing at the motel."

"No," Isla said, grimacing. "Although the vending machine there tried to flirt with me."

Tessa laughed. "So?"

"I rented this tiny blue cottage at the end of Brookmere Road. Cheap, slightly slanted porch, one raccoon, and about four metric tons of dust."

Tessa blinked. "Wait... the blue one with the leaning fence?"

"That's the one."

"Oh, that's *Shamus's* old place. He used to build model boats and leave them in the window like they were trying to escape."

Isla raised an eyebrow. "Well, one of them did. Straight into my forehead. Also, I'm 90% sure the raccoon thought it was the landlord."

Tessa cackled. "Shamus passed a few years ago. His son inherited the place but didn't do much with it. That porch has been tilting since 2003."

"Yeah, it's less porch and more suggestion at this point." Isla leaned back, brushing a stubborn curl off her cheek. "The raccoon hissed at me like I was the intruder."

"Technically, you were."

"I paid rent," Isla muttered. "I should at least get a key and shared custody of the pantry."

Tessa grinned into her coffee. "You going to stay long?"

"I don't know yet." Isla looked down at her mug, thumb tracing the chipped rim. "But I unpacked one bag. That feels like progress."

They sat in a brief pocket of quiet. The diner's hum filled the space around them. Soft clinks of cutlery, the low buzz of conversation, Della calling someone "sweetpea" in a tone that sounded like both a threat and a compliment.

Isla cleared her throat. "Anyway, I need to pick up a few groceries before I end up seasoning pasta with despair. Is the general store still the main place?"

Tessa snorted. "Yep. Amos still runs it. Still refuses to get a barcode scanner. Still grumbles at everyone like we personally ruined his life."

"Good," Isla said. "Wouldn't want the economy or the mood to improve."

Tessa chuckled. "You know he keeps dog treats behind the register?"

"Let me guess," Isla said, deadpan. "For customers who behave."

"You're not wrong."

Isla reached for her mug again, a small smile flickering across her face.

Ashmere might be a little broken.
But at least it was *consistently* broken.

Just as Isla lifted her mug again, the bell over the door gave a squeak, as if announcing someone who *needed* to be announced.

Binnie Quimby breezed in wearing the same sunhat from earlier, now pinned with what looked suspiciously like a plastic hummingbird.

She scanned the diner like a general taking stock of her troops, her gaze briefly landing on Isla and Tessa before lighting up with triumphant glee. She beelined to the counter without breaking stride.

"Della, sweetheart," Binnie called, projecting her voice for maximum splash zone, "can I get a slice of that cherry pie to go? I've got mulch to spread and secrets to keep."

Isla sunk half an inch into the booth.

"Oh, and guess what?" Binnie turned toward the nearest occupied tables, none of whom had asked. "You'll never believe who moved into Shamus's old place! That little blue cottage next to me. Rented, of course. *Isla Winters!*"

Three heads turned. One older man gave Isla a thumbs-up, as if she'd won a prize.

"She's back from the city," Binnie continued, somehow louder now, "and I have a *very strong feeling* this town just got interesting again."

Isla stared into her coffee. "Is it too late to move back to Brooklyn?"

Tessa snorted. "Yes. But I hear the raccoon will take you in."

Binnie scooped up her pie, now boxed neatly with a wax paper liner, and waved a gloved hand toward the booth like she was leaving a press conference.

"Don't be strangers, girls," she called. "And Isla, dear? If you hear strange noises at night, it's probably the wind. Or ghosts. Hard to say."

Then she was gone. Hat, hummingbird, and all.

The door jingled shut behind her.
Isla blinked at it. "Is she always like that?"

"Only on days ending in 'y.'"

Half the diner was now casually glancing her way. They were not staring, just confirming. Satisfied. As if they'd all received their morning dose of gossip from Binnie and, like warm coffee, it would sustain them until lunch.

Chapter 3: General Store

Isla stood just outside the general store, coffee still warming her hand. The glass window was a little fogged in the corner, like even it had trouble seeing clearly some days.

Inside, she could just make out the glow of fluorescent lights, a spinning rack of postcards no one bought, and what appeared to be a single balloon bobbing on a long string like it had lost the will to rise.

She pushed the door open, the little bell above it offering a metallic "ting" that somehow sounded both bored and judgmental.

The store smelled like wood polish, freezer burn, and the faint echo of cinnamon gum. The front half was stocked with everyday groceries: milk, canned beans, soap, cereal. But even here, the packaging looked slightly sun-faded, like everything had aged a few months the moment it entered Ashmere airspace.

Beyond that... was something else.

An entire wall was devoted to what could only be described as *lost trends*. Slinkies in mismatched colors. Half-torn boxes of loom band kits. A hanging row of slap bracelets, their plastic sheen dulled with time. A bucket of yo-yos sat on the floor under a hand-painted sign that read: "YOLO YOYO? $2."

It was like stepping into a garage sale curated by a time traveler who'd given up halfway through the 2010s.

Isla walked slowly down the center aisle, her boots creaking softly against the scuffed linoleum.

She passed a shelf labeled "Wellness," which contained a single bottle of multivitamins, two lavender candles, and a stress ball shaped like a frog wearing a crown.

A rotating sunglasses stand sat nearby, still playing a soft motor hum though half the glasses had long since disappeared. A sticker on its base read: "Amos's Summer Blowout! (2009)"

Half the store was trying to be useful. The other half was a monument to impulse orders gone wrong.

Isla let out a small, amused breath. "Random chaos... but charming," she murmured.

Just then, a loud cough echoed from somewhere behind the counter, followed by the unmistakable clink of a coffee mug on porcelain.

Of course.
Amos Reeve had been here longer than most of the inventory.

A loud throat-clearing cut through the store like a cannon shot in a museum. Then came the slow shuffle of boots on old floorboards, followed by the man himself.

Amos Reeve emerged from behind a leaning tower of paper towels like a relic in motion. Flannel shirt, suspenders, deeply furrowed brow: the kind of face that had been skeptical since birth. A pencil sat behind one ear, though Isla doubted it had moved in years.

He squinted at her for a long moment.

"Well, I'll be," he finally said, voice gravel dragged through molasses. "If it isn't Isla Winters."

"Guilty," she said, lifting a hand.

"You got any news from New York?" he asked, folding his arms across his chest.

He said it with the weight of someone expecting an update from the front lines of the Civil War like she might pull a parchment from her coat and declare troop movements.

Isla blinked. "Lost two horses, but we held the bridge."

Amos gave a single, satisfied nod, like that answered everything.

He moved behind the counter with the grace of a man who'd spent forty years dodging nonsense, or perhaps just Binnie.

"Not much call for news these days," he muttered, turning back toward her as he fiddled with a receipt roll. "Nobody wants to buy local anymore, either. Got folks

29

ordering toothpaste by drone. By *drone*, Isla. Like we're all living in some kind of Jetsons nightmare."

She raised an eyebrow.

"I tell ya, I even started ordering stuff on Amazon just to stock the shelves. Cheaper than the wholesalers." He waved vaguely toward the aisle of slap bracelets and yo-yos, like he expected Bezos himself to peek around the corner.

Then he paused. Realized. Blinked.

"...Not that I should be telling you that."

Isla bit back a smile. "Your secret's safe with me. And the frog-shaped stress ball."

Amos grunted, reaching under the counter for a battered paper bag.

"You need groceries or just a hint of nostalgia?"

"Little of both."

He nodded again. "That's what we sell now. Cereal and time travel."

Isla wandered down the main grocery aisle, grabbing a basket from the stack by the door. It let out a small plastic groan, like even it had opinions.

She moved slowly past the shelves, tossing in a few basics: coffee, a loaf of bread, margarine in a pale-yellow tub that looked like it hadn't changed branding since the 80s. A block of cheddar with slightly fogged plastic went in next. The essentials of survival, or at least something resembling breakfast.

Behind her, Amos's voice floated over the shelves.

"Used to be you could trust your neighbors," he said, not loudly, but with the kind of tone that carried anyway. "Now you lock your shed and hope for the best."

Isla reached for a jar of instant coffee. "You okay back there, Amos?"

He ignored the question, or maybe answered it, just in his own way.

"Had a fella come in last month, an outsider. Asked if I had Wi-Fi. I told him this place barely has *gravity*."

She smirked, tossing a jar of jam into the basket. "Next thing you'll be telling me you accept Bitcoin."

Amos made a sound halfway between a laugh and a cough. "Only thing I accept is cash and low expectations."

Isla glanced down the aisle toward him. He'd returned to his stool behind the counter, leaning back with his arms crossed, looking like a man who trusted neither technology nor optimism.

"You really think things have changed that much?" she asked, loading a carton of eggs into her basket.

Amos didn't answer right away. Just stared out the window like he was waiting for someone to prove him wrong.

"Let's just say," he said finally, "Ashmere used to keep its secrets quiet. Now they just echo louder."

Isla paused by the canned soup, fingers hovering near a dusty label.

She wasn't sure what that meant.

But she was pretty sure he wasn't talking about soup.

Isla stepped out of the general store, the bell behind her giving one last tired jingle like it, too, was ready for a break.

She loaded her groceries into the back seat of the Focus, which responded with a metallic creak that could've been judgment. The eggs wobbled dangerously in their carton. She steadied them with one hand, then closed the trunk with her hip.

That's when she saw him.

Across the street, crouched near the base of an old storefront, a man was repairing the lower edge of a faded wooden frame. He had the kind of presence that didn't announce itself, it just settled in. Rolled-up sleeves, well-worn jeans, tool belt slung low, and a quiet focus that made the whole task seem like it mattered more than it probably did.

He looked up at the sound of her trunk shutting.

Met her eyes.

And gave a small, easy wave.

Not assuming. Just... human.

Isla hesitated, then crossed the street.

"Hey," she said, brushing a bit of windblown hair behind her ear. "Is that your shop?"

He stood up, wiping his hands on a rag. "Nah. Just fixing the trim. Belongs to Mrs. Donnelly. She says the wind makes it 'groan like a haunted ship.' Her words."

"That sounds... accurate."

He smiled. Small, but genuine.

"Mason," he offered. "Wilder. I run a little woodworking shop out near the forest line. Mostly furniture. Sometimes stubborn windows."

"Isla. Winters. I rent raccoon-infested real estate and purchase expired groceries for fun."

Mason's brow lifted, amused. "You must be in the blue cottage."

"Wow. News really does travel fast here."

"Binnie Quimby passed by ten minutes ago with pie and a mission."

Isla rolled her eyes. "Of course she did."

They stood in a brief, companionable silence. The town murmuring around them, the breeze lifting Mason's hair just enough to make him seem like the cover model for a magazine no one admits to reading.

"You from here originally?" he asked.

"Sort of. I left after high school. Came back because...
well. Life happened."

He nodded slowly. "That's usually why people come
back."

Another pause.

"You like it?" she asked, gesturing faintly toward the
street, the town, the view of the river just beyond the
rooftops.

Mason looked out toward the hills, then back at her.

"I do," he said. "It's slow. But it remembers you."

Isla folded her arms gently. "I'm not sure I want to be
remembered yet."

Mason gave her a lopsided half-smile. "Then you
definitely shouldn't have moved next to Binnie."

Isla let the corner of her mouth twitch upward. "Well. I'll
try not to offend the town too much in my first week."

Mason shrugged, adjusting his tool belt. "We've survived
worse. One guy opened a gluten-free hot dog stand.
Lasted two days."

"I'm almost impressed."

"You shouldn't be."

She took a small step back; thumb hooked into her bag
strap. "Nice meeting you, Mason."

"You too, Isla."

She turned and crossed back toward her car, feeling his quiet presence linger behind her like a warm light through a cracked door.

Back at the cottage, Isla slipped the groceries into the fridge, if it could still be called that. The light blinked once, then committed to staying on, and the hum resumed with passive-aggressive volume.

She placed the eggs carefully. The coffee went on the counter. The margarine made a break for freedom and had to be caught mid-roll.

Once everything was vaguely settled, Isla stood for a moment, fingers curled around the edge of the sink, eyes drifting toward the window.

The river had always been her anchor.

Still there. Still moving. Still listening.

She grabbed her hoodie, stepped outside, and let the door creak closed behind her.

It was time to visit the water.

From the cottage, it was only a few streets to the river if you weren't in a hurry. Isla wasn't.

She zipped up her hoodie, tucked her hands into the front pocket, and set off down Brookmere Road, her boots tapping a soft rhythm on the cracked footpath. The air smelled like fallen leaves and distant chimney smoke. It was that soft shoulder season between late summer and early fall, where the light turned golden earlier but the warmth still lingered in pockets.

She passed the Ashmere History Museum: a squat brick building with a faded green awning and a hand-lettered sign reading *Closed Mondays & Always by Accident.* The front windows were dusty, the kind of dusty that looked intentional. Inside, rows of sepia photos stared silently out from crooked frames. Isla slowed just enough to glance at them. Rows of old faces from older times, locked behind glass like they might start whispering if the wind hit just right.

The museum door was locked. A small handwritten note was taped crookedly in the window:
"Back soon (hopefully). – C"

She kept walking.

A block later, the town thinned out. The storefronts gave way to trees, then to river. The Hudson spread out like a shimmering silver ribbon, soft and slow under the afternoon light. A thin mist clung to the far bank, drifting lazily, as if it, too, had nowhere to be.

Isla followed the edge of the path, where wooden benches sat half-sunk into the soil and a pair of ducks quarreled quietly near the reeds. The water moved like breath; steady, shallow, deep where it needed to be.

She paused at a clearing. This was where they used to bring lawn chairs during the summer fireworks. Where she'd once skipped stones and watched them vanish without trace.

The wind lifted her hair gently. She let it.

This place, this town, had always lived half in the past. And for the first time in a long time, that didn't feel like a bad thing.

She slid her phone from her hoodie pocket, thumb brushing the screen.

Twelve missed calls.

All from the same number.
Muted, but still there.
Still trying.

She stared at it, the ache pressing faintly behind her ribs.

He had cheated. Plain and brutal. No excuses, no miscommunications. Just the quiet, hollow horror of knowing that trust had been snapped in half like it hadn't meant a thing. She'd packed a bag in twenty minutes and left the apartment while he was still out. She hadn't looked back.

Until now.
Except she wasn't looking back at *him*. She was looking at something older, something hers.

She locked the screen.
Slipped the phone back into her pocket.

The river didn't care about any of it.

And that, somehow, made her feel safe.

Chapter 4: Museum

The bell above the museum door didn't ring. It *clicked,* like a throat being cleared softly in a chapel.

Isla stepped inside and let the door drift shut behind her. The air was still; the kind of stillness that suggested it had been sitting uninterrupted for some time like the building was exhaling slowly after too many days without visitors.

Dust lingered in beams of light that angled down through high windows, catching on the uneven glass and pooling in corners like forgotten fog. A ticking wall clock kept time in the wrong rhythm; too slow, too loud, and strangely calming.

No one stood at the front desk.

No sound of footsteps. No cheerful greeting. Just the low creak of old floorboards adjusting to her presence.

Isla stood quietly, letting her eyes adjust. The small, one-room museum had always looked bigger in her memory; childhood school visits, the thrill of being somewhere "official" with its glass cases and red velvet ropes. Now, it felt like a shoebox full of echoes.

A wooden placard near the entry read:

Ashmere Historical Society Museum
Est. 1912 Preserving What We Remember.

Below it, a guestbook rested on a podium, half-covered by a promotional flyer for the upcoming Riverside Festival. Isla flipped the guestbook open briefly. The last entry was dated nearly two weeks ago. The signature looked like a child's, or someone trying to disguise theirs.

She moved quietly through the room.

The exhibits were small but earnest. A cracked school bell from 1883. A set of rusted ferry tokens. A faded uniform from the Ashmere Brickworks baseball team, complete with moth holes and a patch sewn on upside-down. Every object had a little printed card beside it, and every card had the same earnest tone: local pride tinged with mild apology.

She stopped at a display of town photos. Three long rows of framed black-and-white images mounted on the wall like a memory parade.

Farmers in overalls, standing in mud beside proud pigs. A group of children in bonnets holding May Day ribbons. A shot of the old train station, now collapsed, with smoke curling above it like a ghost still rising.

Isla took her time.

That was the thing about Ashmere: it asked you to go slow. Even the dust took its time settling.

Toward the far end of the photo wall, one image caught her attention.

It wasn't especially large; just an old 8x10 print in a dark wooden frame. The glass was clean, the photo crisp despite its age. It showed a crumbling estate house, half-choked by trees. Ivy ran wild up one side. The front steps looked uneven. Two top-floor windows had no curtains, just dark squares like watching eyes. The whole structure sat at a slight angle, as if resisting the camera.

There was no label beneath it.

No caption. No date. No description.

Just a blank ivory slot where a card should have gone, or maybe once had.

Isla stepped closer. Tilted her head. Something about the photo made her stomach hum. Not fear, exactly, but that low electrical awareness that something was off and not ready to explain itself.

She leaned in, reading the photo's texture. It was taken in daylight, but the shadows pooled around the porch in strange shapes. The trees behind it were dense, almost blurred at the edges. She couldn't tell if it was just age... or intention.

And maybe that was the part that struck her most.

You don't look abandoned, she thought.
You look like you're waiting.

Behind her, something creaked, soft and deliberate.

Footsteps.

Isla turned, but no one was visible yet. The sound had come from behind a partition near the back half-wall of corkboard and clip frames that shielded a storage area or perhaps a desk.

She stepped away from the photo, suddenly aware of how quiet the place still was. Even the clock had paused, its second-hand twitching in place.

Then a voice, low, female, polite, called out:

"Sorry for the quiet. I wasn't expecting anyone just now. I'll be with you in a moment."

The footsteps grew more defined, approaching from behind the partition.

Isla stepped back toward the center of the room, blinking away the dust that had begun to itch at the corners of her eyes.

A woman appeared around the partition, smoothing a silk scarf as she stepped into view.

She was in her mid-50s, tall and composed, with silver-streaked hair pulled into a low twist that said *I do not forget things.* Her blouse was ivory, not a speck of dust on it, and her boots looked like they'd never met mud. A canvas tote hung neatly from one arm, the kind that said *accessory* more than *shopper.*

"Oh," she said, stopping mid-step when she saw Isla. "I didn't think anyone else was here."

Isla offered a polite smile. "I snuck in under cover of dust."

The woman laughed softly, not startled, not put off. If anything, she seemed mildly pleased.

"Miranda Voss," she said, offering her hand. "I was just dropping off a few items for the museum. Old letters, some newspaper clippings. I donate here regularly. Helps keep the lights on."

Her tone was warm, but the words were selected with surgical precision. *I support this place. It matters because of people like me.*

"Isla Winters," Isla replied, shaking her hand. "Local drifter. Occasional consumer of cinnamon gum and museum silence."

Miranda tilted her head slightly, amusement flickering across her expression. "Winters? As in.."

"Yes," Isla said gently, already knowing what came next. "My parents were Mark and Ellen Winters. We moved away years ago. I just... moved back."

Miranda's expression shifted into something more performative. It was gentle sympathy polished for easy use.

"Of course," she said. "I remember your mother. Lovely woman. Had very grounded opinions about the town council."

Isla smirked faintly. "That sounds like her. She once told a zoning officer he had the critical thinking skills of a wet sponge. I do feel sorry for the staff at the Florida Retirement Village they are living at now."

Miranda let out a smooth laugh that was practiced, but not unkind. "Well, we all need passionate voices."

She glanced toward the photo wall behind Isla. "Reminiscing, or just hiding from the townspeople?"

"A bit of both," Isla said. "I didn't remember that house, though, the one with the trees growing into the roof. It wasn't labelled."

Miranda followed her gaze, but only for a moment.

"Yes, some of those photos came from private collections. We're still organizing them. The curator tends to get... protective about the labels.", pausing. "Some houses, I suppose, prefer to be forgotten."

Isla raised an eyebrow. "That's comforting."

Miranda smiled again, just slightly. "We try to make history hospitable, but it does have its rough corners."

She shifted her tote to the other shoulder.

"Well," she said, brushing a stray thread from her sleeve, "do stop by the museum table at the Riverside Festival. I'm sure Clarissa would love to see some new faces. She's *very* committed to visibility."

"Isn't she the one who gave the gazebo a QR code?"

"She's nothing if not future-focused."

Miranda offered a small nod of farewell; not quite a bow, not quite a dismissal.

"Lovely to meet you, Isla. I'm sure we'll cross paths again."

Then she glided out the door, leaving only the faint scent of rosewater and well-maintained authority behind her.

Isla stood there for a moment longer, then turned back to the photo wall.

Isla stood there a moment longer, eyes drifting back to the photo wall.

She wasn't sure what Miranda had just done. Did she introduce herself or delivered a press release.

Probably both.

She exhaled, gave the unlabeled photo one last look, and muttered under her breath,

"Ashmere: where even the small talk comes with a sponsor."

Then she turned and made her way out, stepping carefully so as not to trip over history on the way out.

Ashmere's main street curved like it had been drawn by someone uncertain about commitment. It made a lazy bend past the museum, the diner, and a few sun-bleached benches that had witnessed generations of small talk and teenage angst.

Chapter 5: Tripping Hazards

Isla stepped out of the museum and into mid-morning light, the kind that made everything look slightly overexposed. The town was quiet again but not silent. A breeze rustled the hanging flower baskets, and somewhere down the block, windchimes did their best impression of how to make strange sounds when tangled up.

She turned toward the corner, hands in her hoodie pocket, not thinking about much at all.

Until a *thud* broke the calm.

Followed by a sharp *"Oof!"* and the unmistakable sound of something or someone trying to recover both balance and dignity at the same time.

From behind a row of sidewalk planters, a tall figure emerged. Slim, lanky, and slightly winded, he wore the full Ashmere deputy uniform like it had been tailored for someone else. The shirt was a shade too bright. The badge caught too much sunlight. And the utility belt clanked with the tragic optimism of someone who truly believed he'd need zip ties today.

He looked about twenty-eight, give or take and with the movements of someone overcaffeinated.

"Hi. umm Isla?" he blurted, pointing at her with a finger that immediately turned into a weird half-salute.

She blinked. "Uh. Yes?"

"Wow. I mean. Whoa. I didn't know you were back. In town. You're here. That's great Hi." He paused to exhale like a balloon deflating sideways. "Sorry, I tripped over a pamphlet box."

He motioned vaguely behind him, as if to indicate the villain of the hour, the curbside planter.

Isla raised an eyebrow. "I see Ashmere law enforcement is as agile as ever."

"Deputy Ronny Patch," he said proudly, brushing imaginary dust off his shoulder and standing up straighter, as if that would erase the stumble. "Well. You probably remember me from school."

She tilted her head. "Were you the one who tried to break into the vending machine with a protractor?"

Ronny's face turned three shades of pink. "That... was an experimental engineering phase."

Isla tried not to smile. She failed, slightly.

Ronny chuckled awkwardly and ran a hand through his hair, which immediately fell back into its previous disarray like even it refused to be policed.

"So, uh... how long you been back?" he asked, clearly trying to sound casual but mostly sounding like someone trying to pronounce *charcuterie* for the first time.

"Just since yesterday," she said. "Rented the little blue cottage on Brookmere."

"Oh," he said, eyes widening like she'd just announced she lived in a lighthouse full of ghosts. "Shamus's old place. That's... brave. Lotta... history."

Isla narrowed her eyes slightly. "History, or raccoons?"

"Same difference in Ashmere," he said with a shrug.

There was a pause.

Ronny shifted his weight from one foot to the other, then suddenly remembered something.

"Oh! Right, that's actually what I was, well, I wasn't *assigned* to tell people, but you know, community presence and all that. The Riverside Festival's on tomorrow night. Kicks off around five. Music, food, those float lantern things Clarissa loves. Should be good."

He offered a hopeful smile. "You going?"

Isla shrugged. "Maybe. Depends if my car starts and if I still have social energy after buying milk."

Ronny grinned, then immediately tried to tone it down, like his own enthusiasm startled him.

"Well... if you go, I'll probably be... around. Official capacity. Crowd safety. Lost children. Policing."

"Sounds like a full docket."

"You'd be surprised."

Another pause.

"Well," Isla said gently, "try not to trip over any more plants, Deputy."

He touched his forehead like he'd seen someone salute once in a movie and decided to keep the dream alive. "Right. Ma'am. Have a good day."

As she walked away, she could feel his eyes on her. It was not in a creepy way, just... like someone realizing his teenage crush had materialized in high definition.

Behind her, it distinctly sounded like Ronny was tripping again.

She didn't turn around.

But she smiled.

Walking down the street, Isla stepped into Riverbend Books.

It smelled like old paper, wood polish, and with what smelt like cat food. Isla wondered if the chubby feline near her cottage ventured this far. The front window held a display of mystery paperbacks arranged in a lopsided pyramid, each with hand-written recommendation tags clipped to them like hopeful name badges, as if they themselves may defeat the burgeoning onslaught of capitalism and scale.

A single string of fairy lights blinked lazily overhead, as if even they weren't quite sure they had the energy.

The shop was narrow but deep, with creaking floorboards and mismatched shelves that leaned into one another like gossiping friends.

Isla paused at the threshold and let the quiet soak in.

This was the kind of quiet that didn't demand anything from you. Not like a phone. Not like people.

She wandered down the main aisle, fingers brushing lightly against spines as she moved. There was biographies, classics, and local authors with suspiciously vague back covers. A few titles she remembered from college. A few she swore she meant to read and never did. In the back, a small handwritten sign declared **Staff Picks** and pointed to a low shelf below the poetry section.

That's where she found it.

A slim novel with a matte navy cover and white serif lettering:
The Quiet Order.

She picked it up, intrigued though mostly by the title. The blurb mentioned memory and secrecy. Sounded like just the right mix of calm and eerie. Perfect for reading in uneven lighting with a bad cup of coffee whilst raccoons were plotting to attack you.

She flipped it open. The pages felt soft, not glossy, not overproduced. Like someone meant it to be held by people who didn't rush.

Sold.

She tucked it under her arm and meandered toward the register, where a young man with square glasses and a slightly overwhelmed expression stood behind the counter. He wore a cardigan that had survived a moth ambush and looked like he'd been given the job against his will.

He glanced up as she approached.

"Hey," he said. "Buying something. Wow. That's... kind of rare."

Isla raised an eyebrow. "I'll try not to make a habit of it."

He cracked a half-smile and rang up the book.

"Most people just browse. Or ask if we sell gift cards. Or think we're a juice bar."

"Do you get a lot of walk-ins looking for kale smoothies?"

"One woman left angry because we didn't stock essential oils."

"Well. You should fix that. Big gap in the market."

He chuckled, slid her book into a brown paper bag, and pushed it across the counter.

"You local?"

"Kind of. Just moved back."

"Ah. So you've already met Binnie."

Isla laughed. "Within twelve minutes of arriving."

"She's the reason we're still open. Bought every single romance novel we had over the summer. Said she was doing 'a private survey.' We didn't ask questions."

"I feel like that *is* the survey."

"Pretty much."

He leaned on the counter, lowering his voice slightly.

"You going to the festival tomorrow night?"

"I heard something about it."

"Big thing around here. Lanterns on the river, food stalls, Clarissa with a megaphone. It's... not terrible."

"That's a glowing review."

"We aim for medium expectations."

He tapped a small stack of flyers beside the register and offered her one. The design was cheerful and slightly chaotic. Pastel colors, bold fonts, clip art lanterns that looked like they'd escaped from a PowerPoint presentation.

Isla took it, folding it in half without much ceremony.

"Thanks."

"Sure. And enjoy the book. That one's weird in a good way."

She paused, gave a small nod, and offered a dry smile.

"Weird in a good way's my type."

Then she slipped out the door, bell jingling once more. Just enough sound to prove she'd been there, even if no one followed.

Chapter 6: Journal

The cottage was quiet except for the occasional pop from the old baseboard heater and the soft whir of the fridge sounding mildly offended to still be working.

Isla sat cross-legged on the lumpy couch, one lamp on beside her, a blanket wrapped around her shoulders out of habit rather than cold. Her duffel bag sat open nearby, clothes half-folded, half falling out, as if slowly unpacking themselves. Beside it, her notebook, the one that had followed her across three apartments and now heartbreak, lay open on her knees.

She hadn't written in it in months.

Maybe years, properly.

But tonight… it felt like time.

She clicked her pen. Hesitated. Then began to write.

Thursday, June 20

I don't really know why I stopped writing.
Actually that's a lie. I do.

Because every time I opened a page, I had to face the fact that I was shrinking.

I moved to New York when I was nineteen. For him.

Not for a dream, or a job, or even myself. Just for a boy with big plans and no alarm clock. He said he needed space to make something of himself. And I thought if I loved him enough, I could be that space.

So, I worked. Hostessing, temping, receptionist gigs, admin jobs with bad lighting and worse coffee. I paid rent. I made dinner. I said I was proud of him when I felt like I was disappearing.

Fifteen years.

Fifteen years of holding the scaffolding of someone else's life, hoping one day he'd build something for us both.

And for most of those years, I believed we'd get married. That it was just a matter of timing. That my patience was romantic and not... sad.

But he never proposed. Never even really answered when I brought it up.

And then, one morning, I found the messages. Casual cheating. Regular cheating. Like I wasn't someone to cherish, just someone convenient to cheat on.

He was out getting bagels. I was halfway packed by the time he came back.

I didn't leave a note. I didn't owe him that.

But somehow, I still owe *me* a new start.

So, I came back here.

Ashmere.

And God, it's strange. Not quiet exactly. Not with Binnie holding court over every fence and Ronny nearly tripping into traffic just to say hi.

But it's... slower.

Less demanding. Less performative. Like I don't have to earn my right to exist here by pretending to be interesting all the time.

There's something comforting in how the people don't rush. How the town isn't trying to sell me something every five minutes. How people remember your name even if they don't know your story.

Got a call from Mum today. Her and Dad are enjoying retirement in Florida. She kept talking about how there was a baby gator sunning itself by the golf course like it paid the HOA fees. I think she was hoping I'd ask about the community pickleball league. I didn't.

Today I bought a book.

I haven't done that in so long. Not for work. Not to impress anyone. Just because the title made me pause. *The Quiet Order*. Maybe I want that. Some kind of quiet order. Not perfection. Just space. Breath. A rhythm I don't have to chase.

I don't know if I'm staying for a long time.

But for now, this place feels like it remembers something
I forgot
how life's supposed to feel.

And for the first time in a long time, I'm not bracing for
the next disappointment.

I'm just... here.

Chapter 7: The Festival

The Ford Focus coughed its way down the final hill like it had caught something from the local wildlife.

Isla winced as the engine gave a wet, gravelly sputter, the mechanical equivalent of a smoker's cough, and coaxed it into a patch of grass that vaguely resembled a parking space.

The tires crunched unevenly as she yanked the handbrake with theatrical caution. The car shuddered once and went quiet. Possibly dead. Possibly resting.

She sighed. "You did your best, bud."

Sliding out, she gave the door a gentle nudge with her hip until it clicked shut. Her reflection in the driver's side window wasn't terrible; the kind of disheveled that suggested a good intention abandoned mid-stride.

Her hair was doing its own thing again, pulled back, but already beginning to rebel. The jeans were less ripped than usual, though still not entirely free of paint smudges from an old apartment job she never finished. Her hoodie had been replaced with a loose cotton jacket that didn't quite match her shoes, but at least she'd remembered both.

The parking job was angled. Not charmingly so. Just...
off.

She gave it one long glance and sighed again. "Close
enough."

Ahead of her, the festival unfolded in flickers and
clustered groups.

The river curved wide and dark beneath a pale sky, its
surface dappled with orange light from the paper
lanterns strung overhead. They hung in long arcs
between wooden poles, swaying slightly in the breeze,
casting warm halos over the gravel footpaths and patches
of grass.

From this distance, the sounds came softly; a hum of
conversation, the occasional bark of laughter, the low
thrum of a folk guitar drifting in and out like radio static
from another decade.

Isla stood still for a moment, hands in her jacket pockets,
just watching.

The festival hadn't fully bloomed yet. It was in that
golden stage where the sky still held a trace of blue and
everyone was just beginning to loosen .People were
starting shed the day and slip into something slower.

Tiny lights traced the outlines of pop-up stalls and tent
awnings near the river's edge. Somewhere near the
docks, a small group of kids darted past a glowing
lantern arch, their sneakers flashing as they vanished into

the dusk. A woman in a sunhat herded them gently back toward the main path, her laughter just audible over the sound of cicadas beginning to tune up.

Isla breathed in.

Grass. Smoke. Fried sugar. A hint of river mud.

This was what summer smelled like in Ashmere. Not curated. Not filtered through glass storefronts or synthetic HVAC.

Just... present.

She adjusted the strap of her crossbody bag, pushed a curl behind her ear that had already returned twice, and took a step forward.

Time to see who and what the night might bring.

Each step Isla took pulled her a little deeper into the festival. From the wide, lantern-lit clearing near the riverbank into the soft, humming maze of pop-up tents and fold-out tables.

The grass beneath her boots was dry in some places, damp in others, and the whole field had the uneven slope of a town that had chosen charm over symmetry.

She passed the kettle corn stand first. Its operator appeared more interested in eating than selling, a bowl balanced precariously on top of the warming drum. Then a booth marked *"Woven Things"* that turned out to be a collection of mismatched scarves and a single crocheted snake with button eyes.

To her left, wind chimes twinkled in the breeze. Some made of glass, others of flatware, one strung entirely from old hotel key tags.

And then she saw her.

Binnie Quimby, across the way, mid-story with a group of women near a folding table stacked with fruit pies. Her sunhat was festooned with something new tonight; what looked like a paper sunflower taped on last-minute. Her hands moved with theatrical rhythm as she spoke.

Isla couldn't hear the words, but she could tell it was *something*. Binnie's audience leaned in, laughing, one of them gasping with an open-mouthed hand flutter. Classic Binnie: half information, half performance, all crowd control.

Isla smiled to herself and drifted on.

Just as she passed a candle stall with scents ranging from *River Fog* to the more mysterious *Porch Memory,* she caught movement from the corner of her eye.

Ronny Patch.

He was stationed beside a laminated poster for "Festival Safety Tips," clutching a half-full soda like it might explode. His uniform was less wrinkled than usual, but still gave the distinct impression it had been put on in a hurry and a size too small.

He spotted her.

His face lit up too quickly, and he raised a hand in what might've started as a wave but turned into something more like a startled salute. The gesture stalled halfway, then awkwardly resumed; a flick, then a point, then a nervous sip of his soda like he hoped it might erase the last three seconds.

The sip resulted in Ronny spilling part of it onto his boot.

Isla gave a polite nod in return, her smile tugging wider as she turned away.

Just past the food vendors, she noticed a modest stall set slightly apart. A single fold-out table, clean but unadorned, topped with trays of small, glinting items. Coins. Stamps. Labelled with perfect block lettering and low prices.

Behind it sat **Amos Reeve**, cross-armed, frowning like someone had just suggested hip hop was music.

He didn't look up as Isla passed, but one hand hovered near a portable cash box like he expected someone, somewhere, to try something.

The table bore a hand-painted sign:

Local History, Coins and Stamps. Ask Before Touching. Don't Haggle.

Beside it, a second sign, scribbled in red Sharpie:

No, they're not chocolate coins. Don't ask again.

Isla slowed for a moment. Not enough to engage. Just enough to admire the dedication to grumpiness as an art form.

The scent of grilled corn and sweet cider carried through the air, mixing with wood smoke and grass.

She let herself meander, eyes soft, pace unhurried.

The festival didn't push. There were no loud sales tactics here. It just moved around her. Lanterns flickering, laughter rising and falling, familiar faces appearing like motifs in a town-sized painting.

Chapter 8: Lemonade

Tessa Blake caught sight of her from behind the lemonade stand and waved like she'd been waiting for this moment all evening. She ducked around the stall, two paper cups in hand, and led Isla toward a plastic table setup under a string of flickering bulbs.

The chairs looked like the kind that had lived several lives. White, stackable, slightly sunken in the middle, and the table rocked just enough to make them both hesitate before sitting, sinking slightly into the soft soil.

They clinked their paper cups in mock ceremony.

"To... Ashmere nightlife?" Tessa offered.

"To not falling through the chair," Isla replied.

They drank. The lemonade was tart enough to feel like a small warning.

"So," Tessa said, eyeing her over the rim of the cup, "I saw you get spotted by our very own Deputy Ronny Patch."

"Oh, I was *definitely* spotted," Isla said. "There was a wave, a salute, a near-soda-related incident... I think I'm engaged now."

Tessa burst out laughing. "Poor Ronny. He's had that same deer-in-headlights expression since tenth grade. Honestly, he used to blush when people said *traffic violation*."

"Still does," Isla said. "I think I saw him trying to arrest a wasp earlier."

Tessa wiped a tear from her eye. "He means well. But I don't know how he graduated from basic training without tripping into a drainage ditch."

They both sipped, letting the breeze move around them for a minute, the warm air brushed with music and distant laughter.

"Actually," Isla said after a pause, "I ran into someone else, too. Mason Wilder?"

Tessa raised an eyebrow. "Oh, the quiet lumber prince?"

"More like woodworking cryptid. Fixed something outside the old Donnelly shop. Seemed... nice."

"He *is* nice," Tessa said, drawing out the word with mild suspicion. "Also not married, in case that's your next question."

"I wasn't going to ask," Isla said, deadpan.

"But you were wondering."

"Maybe."

Tessa leaned back in her chair. "He keeps to himself. Lives out near the trailhead. Builds beautiful furniture, helps old ladies fix fences, never says no to a stray animal or a community fundraiser. Very mysterious, very capable. Basically, the opposite of everyone you dated in your twenties."

Isla raised her lemonade cup. "High bar."

They both smiled.

Tessa took a final sip and stood, brushing imaginary dust from her jeans. "I've got to go help at the jam judging tent. Prevent any disagreements from getting to New York Times level."

Oh, I think the day Ashmere gets in the NYT it will be due to a crossword clue."

As Tessa disappeared into the crowd, Isla sat back in her chair, scanning the path ahead.

And of course, as if right on cue Mason Wilder passed by.

Rolled-up sleeves. Tool belt slung casually. Talking to someone with that same even tone as if he'd never once tripped over his words or spilled anything down his shirt.

He caught Isla's eye mid-sentence and gave a small, easy nod.

She smiled back. Not quite sure what her face was doing, but aware it probably wasn't helping.

After he passed, she looked back down at her almost empty cup.

"I need stronger lemonade," she muttered.

The buzz of the crowd shifted; not louder, just more focused. Conversations dipped, a guitar nearby quieted mid-chord, and a microphone somewhere near the main stage gave a soft feedback squeal.

Isla stayed seated, her cup now mostly ice, as a spotlight flicked on near the riverside platform, more a raised deck with bunting than an actual stage, but it did the job.

Clarissa Finch stepped up to the mic, smiling like a candidate on election night.

Her hair was shellacked into place, her lipstick precise, her blazer too crisp for the humidity. The light caught on the rhinestone Ashmere pin at her collar, which somehow sparkled even though the sun had already dipped below the tree line.

"Good evening, everyone," she began, voice smooth and measured. "For those of you I haven't had the pleasure of meeting me, I'm Clarissa Finch, your local representative on the town council."

There it was. The line landed like a tagline rehearsed in a mirror.

"I want to thank you all for making this year's Ashmere Riverside Festival one of the best yet. From the lantern volunteers to the stall owners, the musicians and performers, your efforts reflect the heart of our community."

She beamed, scanning the crowd like someone waiting for camera flashes.

"We may be small," she continued, "but that doesn't mean we think small. Events like this remind people that Ashmere isn't just a dot on the map. We are a place of tradition, creativity, and forward-thinking spirit."

Isla raised an eyebrow slightly and leaned back in her chair.

Clarissa's speech ticked every box: gratitude, unity, ambition wrapped in floral stationery. It wasn't bad. But it wasn't really for the people standing there. It was for *somewhere else*. A paper trail. A headline. A pitch deck to a greater political office.

Behind Clarissa, a volunteer adjusted one of the lantern poles. Another staffer handed out folded programs to no one in particular. The moment had structure and Clarissa made sure it stayed that way.

"If we continue to support each other, share our stories, and celebrate what makes this town special," she said, "I truly believe Ashmere can shine brighter than ever."

Polite applause followed. Not thunderous, but acceptable. Enough to satisfy a councilwoman. Not enough to require a second microphone check or encore performance.

Clarissa gave a practiced nod and stepped down, heels clicking confidently against the wooden planks.

As the lights dimmed and chatter resumed, Isla stirred her cup with her straw and murmured to herself:

"Well. That was... municipally ambitious."

The crowd had begun to swell again, lanterns glowing brighter now against the deepening dusk, voices rising in loose clusters as the pie judging wrapped and a local band strummed their opening chords somewhere near the main path.

Isla remained seated, her paper cup now empty, the ice inside reduced to vague intention.

She let her gaze drift from the lights overhead to the families shuffling between booths to the lazy curve of the river just beyond the footpath.

And then she saw it.

A figure moving the wrong way.

Not frantic. Not obvious. Just... deliberate.

While the crowd ambled toward the music, this person, tall, jacketed, head slightly bowed was walking against it. They weaved between vendors and picnic tables without hesitation, cutting a path back toward the darker edge of the festival near the cluster of utility tents and garbage bins.

Isla blinked, adjusting her focus.

The figure disappeared behind a tall booth with a canvas sign that read *Artisan Syrups – Small Batches, Big Feelings* and didn't re-emerge.

She sat forward slightly, eyes narrowed.

It could've been nothing. Someone forgot their keys. Staff heading to grab something. Or just a local with bad spatial awareness.

But a few seconds later, she heard it.

Low voices. Not yelling, but close.

Two people. One sharper, the other harder to place.

"...told you this wasn't the time"

"...you said it wouldn't matter"

Then silence.

She waited. Held her breath without meaning to.

Nothing.

Just the hum of the music picking up again, and a teenage girl nearby loudly debating whether lemonade counted as "hydration."

Isla sat back, one eyebrow lifted.

No one else seemed to notice. Or care.

She stared at the Artisan Syrups stall for another moment, but the canvas didn't move. No one came out. No sign of the two voices.

Eventually, she stood, tossed her empty cup in the nearby bin, and turned slowly toward the heart of the festival.

If something was off... it wasn't ready to be seen yet.

The river had gone quiet. Not still, exactly, but hushed. As if even the current was holding its breath.

Clusters of people gathered along the bank where volunteers passed out thin paper lanterns with flickering tea lights inside. Some glowed soft amber, others pale rose or green, and they floated like small stars waiting to be let go.

Isla stood near the edge of the crowd, holding a lantern by its base, thumb brushing against the wax through the paper. The air had cooled just enough to raise goosebumps, but not enough to bother finding a jacket.

"Has anyone seen Deputy Ronny?" Tessa asked, slipping beside her with her own lantern. "Amos is convinced a teenager swiped one of his coins, and apparently Ronny was last seen muttering about conducting a sting operation behind the cider tent."

Isla gave her a sideways glance. "I assume the coin is worth approximately seventeen cents?"

"Sentimental value. Which Amos has in spades. And also rage."

They shared a grin, but were interrupted by the unmistakable sound of sensible shoes and disapproval approaching at speed.

Binnie Quimby appeared between them like a summoned thought, hat askew, cheeks slightly flushed from movement and perhaps cider.

"Ladies," she said breathlessly. "You're both far too calm. That's always a dangerous sign."

"Hi, Binnie," Tessa said wearily.

Binnie ignored the tone entirely, eyes flitting between their lanterns and the crowd gathering at the edge of the water.

"I assume you heard her little speech earlier?" she asked.

"Clarissa?" Isla asked.

"She's not to be trusted, that one," Binnie said, with the certainty of someone relaying gospel truth. "Wants Ashmere in brochures, on travel blogs, with hashtags. She'd sell the cemetery for a press release if she thought the lighting was good enough."

"She's enthusiastic," Tessa offered.

"She's *calculating*," Binnie corrected. "Those are different. Enthusiastic people wear Crocs. Calculating people wear kitten heels to riverfront soil."

Isla tried not to laugh. She failed slightly.

"She used to borrow sugar from my sister and never returned the Tupperware. That's all I'll say."

"That's *not* all you'll say," Isla muttered under her breath.

A hush rippled through the crowd as the signal was given. People knelt by the bank or waded a few steps into the water. One by one, lanterns were lowered, flickering, trembling slightly, and let go.

The river caught them.

Some turned in lazy circles. Others drifted straight, confident, glowing silently as they floated downstream. A few snagged-on reeds, their lights still burning stubbornly as if they refused to be left behind.

Isla watched her own lantern bob, then right itself.

Tessa exhaled. "I forgot how pretty this part is."

Binnie, briefly softened, nodded. "It's the only moment Ashmere keeps its mouth shut."

The water lit up in scattered color, a long breath of light stretching away with the current. Behind them, conversations began again, but quieter now. Less bustle. Fewer people. A shift in energy.

The night had turned.

And something, though they didn't know it yet, had already begun to break loose.

The festival was all but over.

Most of the stalls were packed down into crates and canvas bags, tables folded, signs taken down with mild regret or mild relief depending on the vendor. Only a few lanterns still glowed softly along the riverside, their flicker now more decorative than necessary.

Isla was helping Tessa fold the last few plastic chairs, stacking them in uneven towers near the booth.

The grass beneath their feet was flattened in places, and the breeze had picked up. It was not cold, but enough to tug gently at sleeves and stir the paper napkins that had escaped cleanup.

"That was smoother than I expected," Tessa said, wiping her hands on her jeans. "No pie-related injuries, only one kid lost and recovered within twelve minutes, and I only had to talk to Clarissa twice."

"Impressive," Isla said, clicking the chair legs into place with a satisfying snap. "You didn't even throw lemonade at her."

"Growth," Tessa said dryly. "Or exhaustion."

They both laughed, softly, the way people do when it's late and the night has already told most of its stories.

Chapter 9: A Scream

Isla stretched her back, looking out across the grass toward the river's edge. A few silhouettes still wandered nearby, mostly volunteers wrapping cables or checking trash bins.

Then it happened.

A sharp, clear scream cut across the dark.

Not playful. Not exaggerated. A real scream. The kind that silences conversation like a glass shattering in a quiet room.

Isla and Tessa froze, exchanging a glance.

"Was that?" Isla began.

Tessa was already moving.

They jogged down the slope toward the river path, the grass damp underfoot, chairs forgotten behind them.

More lanterns had burned out now, leaving long shadows and soft pools of light along the water's edge.

Near one of the old stone benches that overlooked the river, a figure stood shaking. Della Jean, one hand pressed over her mouth, the other pointing down toward the rocks.

Isla followed her line of sight.

At the edge of the river, half-draped over the muddy bank, was the body of a woman.

Her hair fanned around her like seaweed. Her shoes were gone. One hand was curled against her side as if she'd simply stopped to rest and never got back up.

The water lapped gently against her coat, moving her just slightly with the current enough to make it look like she might still be breathing.

But she wasn't.

And everyone standing there knew it.
The quiet broke apart like a dropped plate.

Della Jean stood frozen, one hand still over her mouth, the other slightly raised as if trying to hold the moment still. Her face had gone pale beneath her earrings, and she kept blinking like she might unsee what she'd seen.

Tessa reached her first. "Della hey hey, it's okay. Come sit down."

"I, she's…" Della shook her head. "I thought maybe she slipped, or, she was just there, like she'd washed in… but no. No one looks like that if they're alive."

"Deep breaths," Tessa said, guiding her gently toward the bench.

A few more footsteps thudded across the grass. Binnie Quimby arrived with surprising speed for someone who'd claimed earlier her left knee "acted up in humidity."

"Oh, *my word,*" she breathed, skidding to a halt at the top of the slope. "Is that? Is she?" She turned to no one in particular. "I *knew* something was off with the river this year. I said it in March. Didn't I say it in March?"

"Binnie, *not now,*" Tessa snapped.

Miranda Voss appeared next, hands folded neatly in front of her, calm as moonlight. "What happened?"

"She's dead," Isla said softly. "Whoever she is."

Miranda didn't flinch. Just looked at the body with a quiet, clinical frown. "Is someone calling Ronny?"

As if summoned by name and a poor sense of timing, Deputy Ronny Patch jogged breathlessly down the hill, flashlight already on despite the lanterns still glowing all around.

"Nobody move," he said, trying to sound authoritative while gasping for air. "And please don't touch the body. Or anything near it. Or each other."

Tessa raised an eyebrow. "Solid start."

He approached the body with awkward reverence, stopping short of the waterline. He bent down, placing two fingers gently at the neck to check for a pulse, though everyone present already knew what he'd find.

"Do we know who she is?" he asked, mostly to the air.

No one answered at first. Then Miranda stepped forward, squinting in the low light.

"Wait..." she murmured. "That's... Meryl Hartley. She was helping with the historical booth earlier. Quiet woman. Local, but kept to herself."

"Is it? Are you sure?" Tessa asked.

"Yes," Miranda said. "She wore that same cardigan to last month's preservation meeting. It had those pearl buttons."

They all stared again. The body lay still, one arm crooked beneath her side, her head turned slightly away.

"Shouldn't we... cover her or something?" Tessa whispered.

"Don't touch her," Ronny said, stepping forward and almost tripping on a rock. "Crime scene protocol. I'll, uh secure the area."

"With what?" Binnie asked. "Your flashlight and moral authority?"

"Does anyone know what happened?" Ronny pressed, ignoring her.

"I just found her like that," Della murmured from the bench. "I was walking the path saw something at the edge. I thought it was a trash bag at first. God. Her poor face."

"She doesn't look hurt," Isla said quietly.

Everyone looked at her.

She didn't elaborate. Not yet.

A moment passed.

Then someone, a young man still lingering near the cider booth called out from the hill: "Where's Clarissa?"

The question hung there.

Nobody answered.

Miranda didn't blink, but Isla thought she saw the slightest tightening around her mouth.

Tessa looked over at Isla. "What are you thinking?"

Isla took a step closer to the body. Not enough to interfere. Just enough to see better.

The woman's cardigan was buttoned neatly. Her shoes were missing. One earring had come loose, but the other still dangled in place.

But what caught Isla's eye was the glove.

Just one: soft brown leather, still fitted snugly over the right hand. The left was bare.

She glanced around. No one else seemed to notice.

"Odd," Binnie muttered nearby, arms crossed tight over her chest. "Who wears gloves in summer? Strange woman."

Isla didn't answer.

It wasn't the glove itself. It was the *fact* of it. Like someone had started dressing her for something else... and stopped halfway.

It didn't look like a drowning.

It looked like someone had tried to make it *look* like one.

Most of the stalls were already gone.

The lights still swayed overhead, but the booths had been folded away, tables stacked, extension cords coiled like sleeping snakes. Even the cider tent was half-dismantled, its vinyl flaps dragging in the grass.

A few dozen people remained; not festival-goers anymore, just townsfolk who hadn't figured out how to leave yet. They stood in small groups at the edge of the path, voices low, eyes flicking toward the river where the body had been found.

The out of towners had long since left, for their commutes back to the city.

Ronny Patch stepped up onto a wooden pallet someone had left near the power supply box. His flashlight flicked wildly as he adjusted it under one arm, then tried to raise his voice over the wind and mutter of the crowd.

"Okay uh folks?"

A few people looked his way. Most didn't.

He cleared his throat and tried again. "If I could just get your attention for a moment."

Isla turned from where she stood near Tessa, watching him with quiet interest.

"We're going to ask everyone to head home now," Ronny said, voice strained but trying. "The festival's over, and we've had... an incident near the riverbank that we need to investigate."

A woman near the folding chair stack asked, "What kind of incident?"

Ronny hesitated, then, realizing there wasn't a gentler way to say it, delivered the truth like someone reporting a weather warning.

"A body was found. Near the water. The individual is... deceased. There's no danger to the public at this time, but we're treating it as an active situation."

That got their attention. Heads turned. A murmur rippled out like a dropped pebble.

"Who was it?" someone asked. "Was it that woman from the history booth?"

Ronny raised his hand, unsure what to do with it once it was in the air. "We're not confirming anything yet. Please, just... if you saw anything strange tonight, anything out of the ordinary, we'd appreciate it if you came by the station tomorrow."

From behind Isla, Binnie whispered as audibly as ever, "Someone's already posted it to the family group chat. Word's halfway to Delaware by now."

"Let's not spread speculation," Ronny added, glancing toward the whispering.

Another voice piped up from the side. "Where's Clarissa? Wasn't she organizing this?"

Ronny looked around as if expecting Clarissa to emerge from a stall like a politician on cue. She didn't.

"Not sure," he said. "But this isn't a council thing now, this is a police matter."

The remaining townspeople began to drift, slowly, uneasily, toward their cars or the gravel path leading back to Main Street. No rushing. Just that quiet, communal uncertainty that always followed bad news in small places.

The music was gone. The lights were dimming. Only the river moved now, its flow steady, unfazed.

Isla stood in place a moment longer, watching faces, not footsteps.

Everyone was disturbed.

But not everyone looked surprised.

Chapter 10: After

The Ashmere Diner smelled like coffee, maple syrup, and yesterday's news; which, in this case, was literal.

Isla sat across from Tessa in their usual booth by the window, half a cinnamon raisin bagel going cold on her plate. Her coffee steamed lazily beside it, untouched.

The diner wasn't packed, but it buzzed. The kind of low murmur that only happens in small towns when something bad has happened and nobody wants to be the first to say it too loud.

Della Jean was moving from table to table with a pot of coffee in one hand and a story in the other.

"I swear to you," she was saying to a pair of retirees near the counter, "her eyes were *wide open*. Like she saw something. I mean, I didn't touch her. I've watched enough true crime to know *that's a no*, but she looked... *aware*, you know?"

At the booth beside Isla, Binnie Quimby sat with a dry English muffin and an open book, pretending to read while clearly listening to every word.

Tessa leaned over her plate and whispered, "That story gets a little more dramatic every time she tells it. Earlier it was 'washed up and peaceful.' Now it's 'wide-eyed and haunted.'"

Isla stirred her coffee. "Give it two hours and she'll say the ghost winked at her."

Across the room, the bell above the door gave a sharp *ding*. Amos Reeve shuffled in wearing his same brown jacket, hands stuffed in the pockets, expression somewhere between grim and resigned.

Della moved toward him with the reflexes of a server who didn't need to ask his order.

"Got your usual ready to go," she said, setting a takeout bag on the counter.

Amos gave a grunt of thanks, then turned toward the room like he had one more line in him, which he did.

"No good will come from all this gossip," he muttered. "But if you ask me, someone should talk to Clarissa."

That got attention.

He didn't elaborate, just adjusted his grip on the bag and added, almost as an afterthought: "Meryl helped her on the last council election. Pretty closely, too."

Then he turned and walked out.

Della blinked. "Well. He's cheerful today."

Binnie's eyes darted. Taking it all in to recount to others.

Tessa frowned slightly. "Why would he bring up Clarissa like that?"

Isla didn't answer right away. She watched Binnie. Watched Della retell. Watched everyone work so hard to fill the silence.

Then, softly: "I think Ashmere's more careful than it looks."

Tessa frowned. "What do you mean?"

"I mean..." Isla pushed her coffee aside, leaning back. "Nobody's surprised that something happened. Just surprised it happened to *her.*"

Tessa didn't say anything to that. She just picked up her fork and slowly swirled it through the syrup on her plate.

And the diner buzzed on.

The bell above the diner door gave its usual half-hearted jingle as Isla stepped out, the morning sun warming the sidewalk in soft patches.

She'd barely taken three steps when she nearly bumped into someone coming the other way.

Mason Wilder.

Hands in his jacket pockets, tool belt slung low, hair slightly windblown like he'd come straight from doing something practical.

"Hey," he said, pausing. "You hear the news?"

Isla gave him a look. "I was there. I saw the body."

He blinked, surprised. "Seriously?"

"Seriously." She stepped aside so he could pass, but he lingered. "They're calling it a drowning."

Mason tilted his head slightly. "But you're not sure."

"I'm not sure," Isla said. "It didn't sit right."

He nodded once, thoughtful.

"I saw Meryl Hartley the other day," he said. "Monday, I think. She was having a pretty heated argument with Hank Delaney."

Isla's eyebrows lifted. "The old ranger guy?"

"Yeah. I was working on a porch railing two houses down. Couldn't hear what they were saying, but the body language was clear. Arms waving. Hank looked... upset. Not his usual cryptic-old-man mood."

"Do they know each other?"

"No idea. But it wasn't casual."

They stood in a moment of quiet, the town around them already slipping back into its usual routines, deliveries humming past, someone sweeping a shopfront, a dog barking down the block.

"You think it's worth talking to him?" Isla asked.

Mason shrugged gently. "Might be nothing."

"Or something."

He gave a small, crooked smile. "Ashmere's full of those."

Then he stepped past her and into the diner.

Isla watched the door close behind him, her mind already beginning to turn.

Chapter 11: Hank

The river looked different in daylight.

Still slow. Still wide. But less like a mirror and more like a question.

Isla followed the path back down from the town's edge, boots pressing gently into the softened dirt where last night's lantern launch had left faint footprints and flattened grass. The scent of dew and sun-warmed leaves carried on the air, along with a distant woodsmoke curl she couldn't quite place.

The spot where Meryl had been found wasn't marked. No caution tape. No police cones. Just the same bend in the path, the same half-submerged stones near the water's edge.

You could walk past it and never know.

She paused, standing just far enough back not to feel invasive, but close enough to look.

There was nothing to see. No answers left behind. Just a cool breeze off the water and a single dragonfly skimming low across the surface.

She turned from the river and headed farther down the trail, a winding stretch flanked by trees and overgrown fence posts, where the town thinned out and the woods began to lean in.

Hank Delaney's place sat just beyond the turn; a weathered cottage with wood siding faded to silver, nestled in a pocket of trees that seemed to have grown around it rather than beside it. A wind chime made of spoons clinked lazily by the porch.

Isla hesitated at the gate. It hung crooked on its hinges, half-open like it couldn't decide whether to welcome or warn.

She stepped through anyway.

The porch creaked as she climbed it, and before she could knock, a voice called from inside.

"Don't often get visitors before lunch."

It wasn't hostile. Just matter-of-fact. Like the house had spoken through him.

Isla stepped to the doorway, peering through the screen.

Hank Delaney sat in a chair near the hearth, back straight, eyes sharp beneath his greying brow. He wore a wool cardigan over a flannel shirt despite the warming day, and had the posture of a man who knew when he was being watched.

"I'm just here to ask a question". Isla said.

"I was at the festival," she said. "When they found Meryl."

Hank nodded slowly. "Bad thing. Real bad."

"You knew her?"

He looked toward the window. "Everyone knows everyone. That's what makes this place work."

Or fall apart, Isla thought.

"I heard you and Meryl had a conversation recently. Sounded serious."

That got a longer pause.

He didn't look angry. Just old in a way that had nothing to do with age. Tired of being measured for meaning in every sentence.

"You got something to ask, you go ahead and ask it. I know you growing up Isla you always were a curious sort even then." he said.

Isla hesitated.

Then: "Were you arguing with her?"

Hank didn't move. Just tapped the arm of his chair once, slowly.

"We disagreed," he said. "That happens."

"About what?"

"Nothing worth shouting over now."

"That sounds like something worth shouting over then."

He gave a faint, humorless smile. "Smart mouth. You get that from your mother?"

"Probably."

The wind shifted outside, brushing through the trees like an ominous sign.

"Just so you know," Isla said, "I don't think she drowned by accident."

Hank didn't respond.

He just sat there, still as old stone, letting the words settle like dust.

Then he said:

"You ought to be careful what you start turning over in this town. Roots run deep."

She didn't answer.

Didn't need to.

She already knew she was going to turn them anyway.

By the time Isla got back to the blue cottage, the sun had shifted low enough to throw long shadows across the porch. The wind had picked up just enough to make the screen door wheeze again, like it was sighing at her choices.

She dropped her bag on the hall table and kicked off her boots with one landing upright, the other surrendered sideways. She didn't bother correcting it.

The air inside was still a little musty, like the walls hadn't quite decided if she was staying. A faint herbal note lingered from the candle she'd lit the night before, which had now burned down into a waxy crater.

She flicked the light switch.

Nothing.

She flicked it again.

Still nothing.

"Well, that's promising," she muttered, walking to the kitchen and thumping the side of the fridge like she was burping a reluctant baby. It hummed back to life, grudgingly.

Then came the sound.

A scrabble. Soft at first, then more insistent: claws on wood, maybe the porch railing or the side window screen. A pause. Then a thump, like something launching its full body weight against a surface it didn't understand but *very much* intended to overcome.

Isla froze.

"Oh no," she said aloud. "Not again."

She tiptoed toward the front door and peered through the peephole, which was mostly fogged from age. A small, furry blur paced along the edge of the porch.

Another thump.

This time, it came from the side window.

Isla moved to the curtain and peeked through.

There it was the *raccoon*. Or *a* raccoon. She was starting to suspect it was the *same* one. Same bold stare. Same slight limp. Same attitude.

It was perched on the window ledge like it had *paid rent*.

She knocked on the glass.

The raccoon blinked at her. Then licked the pane. Slowly. Like it was challenging her to a duel.

"Absolutely not," she said, drawing the curtain closed with finality.

From outside: a soft, deliberate tap on the window again.

"You're not getting in," she called. "I already have enough chaos in this house. You don't get to be part of my emotional journey."

The raccoon didn't respond obviously. But she could *feel* its judgment.

Isla sighed, poured herself a glass of water, and leaned against the counter.

The lights flickered once then back on.

Small victory.

Outside, the tapping stopped.

Inside, for now, it was just her, the hum of the stubborn fridge, and the growing certainty that this raccoon was now her most committed relationship.

The raccoon had retreated, or at least paused its siege.

Isla sank onto the couch, legs curled beneath her, the glass of water balanced on the armrest like a fragile truce. The sky outside was turning to that soft, pearled grey that came before sunset in Ashmere. There were no harsh lines, just a gentle blur between day and whatever came next.

She reached for her phone and thumbed to her favorites.

Mum.

Two rings.

Then: "Darling! Are you alive? Your father thinks you've been eaten by a bear."

"I'm fine," Isla said, smiling despite herself. "No bears. Just a raccoon with abandonment issues."

"Sounds like your twenties."

"Mum", Isla replied, laughing.

Then Isla's voice softened. "Something happened last night. At the festival."

"Oh?"

"There was a body. A woman, Meryl Hartley. I was there when they found her."

Silence, then a shift in tone. Still gentle, but more alert.

"Meryl Hartley," her mother repeated. "I knew her growing up, a little. Quiet girl, smart as anything. Always nose-deep in some archive. I think she took over the

Historical Society from old June Appleby, remember her?"

Isla didn't, but she nodded anyway.

"Kept everything, that one. Meryl, I mean. Photos, letters, maps... she once came by our house looking for any documents from the flood in '68. Said the town needed to remember more than it forgot."

"Sounds familiar," Isla murmured.

Her mum hummed. "It's strange. I haven't thought about her in years. She really passed?"

"Yeah."

"She was younger than me. Hmph."

Then her mother continued breezily, "Well anyway, the ninth hole's closed today, and it's annoying your father. He won't stop talking about the damn gators. Claims he saw one sunbathing near the cart path. I told him it was probably a very still squirrel, but you know how he is."

Isla laughed softly. "Florida sounds peaceful."

"Oh, it is. Apart from the reptilian warfare."

"You try to stay uneaten mum."

They exchanged a few more words; light, everyday ones, before hanging up. The kind that didn't change anything but reminded you someone still knew your voice.

Isla set the phone down and leaned her head back against the couch.

Meryl Hartley. Photos. Documents. The town's memory in boxes.

And now silence.

But Isla couldn't help but wonder who else had been trying to forget.

Chapter 12: Past and Present

The Ashmere Historical Society Museum was quiet, but not locked.

The front door sat just shy of closed, like someone had let it swing back without catching the latch. A single car idled at the curb; sleek, black, and far too polished for this end of town.

Isla stepped up onto the porch and pushed the door open gently. The faint smell of old wood and older paper greeted her again, the same familiar hush as before. Part reverence, part neglect.

Something about the place had stuck with her. Maybe it was the quiet. Or the photo of the house that still hadn't been labelled.

She was halfway through the foyer when she heard the shuffle of movement ahead. Quick, deliberate.

Miranda Voss appeared from the far hallway, arms full of a cardboard file box, heels clicking far too efficiently for such a sleepy building.

"Oh," she said, startled. "Isla. I didn't realize anyone else would be here."

Isla raised an eyebrow. "Didn't know you for the archiving type."

Miranda gave a tight smile. "Just helping out. The Historical Society board asked for volunteers to sort through Meryl's materials. Thought I'd do my part."

Her voice was smooth, practiced. Hair perfect. Nails untouched by cardboard.

"Generous of you," Isla said, glancing toward the box. It was unmarked except for a slanted post it note: *M.H. - COUNCIL - CORRESP.*

Miranda noticed the glance and subtly shifted the box in her arms. "She had so much clutter. Letters, drafts, meeting notes from the nineties... most of it barely legible. Her family won't know what to do with it."

Isla nodded, stepping just slightly closer. "Figured the Society would keep those things in case they were important."

"Oh, I'm only taking a few to sort through," Miranda said quickly. "I'll bring anything relevant back, of course."

Miranda adjusted her grip again, clearly ready to leave.

"Best to keep things orderly in times like these," she added, more to herself than Isla.

"Sure," Isla said. "Just make sure nothing important gets lost."

Their eyes met just briefly and Isla held the look long enough to feel the edge of something unsaid.

Then Miranda smiled again. "Have a good day."

She stepped past and disappeared through the door, the click of her heels fading into the sidewalk.

Isla turned back to the hallway.

The museum was still. But the shelves looked slightly disturbed; a gap where a row of folders had been, a drawer half-shut, a pencil left rolling near the edge of a desk.

She crossed to the display wall. The photo was still there, the unlabeled one. Sepia-toned, slightly curled at the corners, tucked between two better-documented prints with dates and names in careful handwriting.

The house looked familiar and out of place all at once. Perhaps Ilsa had seen it as a child, she thought, but long since forgotten where. It was grand but weathered, set back behind trees that now might not even exist.

Isla stared at it for a long moment.

Then pulled out her phone and snapped a quiet photo.

No flash. No sound. Just one click.

She tucked the phone back in her jacket pocket.

Not because she had a theory.
Not yet.

Just because she'd learned to keep things that didn't quite fit.

Isla stepped out of the Ashmere Historical Society Museum and let the door fall shut behind her with a soft thud.

The sunlight had shifted. It was later now, slanting long and golden across the sidewalk, brushing against the cracked paint of the porch railings and the old picket fence that had definitely seen better decades.

She was halfway down the steps when she heard a familiar voice.

"Twice in one day. People will talk."

She turned.

Mason Wilder stood on the sidewalk, toolbox in one hand, the other shading his eyes as he looked up at her. A smudge of paint trailed across his forearm, and his hair had taken on the mild chaos of someone who hadn't expected to see anyone important.

"Let me guess," Isla said. "Routine maintenance on a century-old door that never quite shuts?"

He grinned. "Got asked to look at the back lock. Probably hasn't been changed since Nixon."

They stood a moment, neither rushing.

Then Isla reached into her jacket pocket and pulled out her phone. "Hey, quick question."

"That's usually how it starts," Mason said, stepping closer.

She showed him the screen. The photo she'd just taken; grainy, unlabeled. The house behind the trees.

"You recognize this place?"

Mason leaned in slightly, squinting. "Huh."

A pause.

"I don't know the name, but that roofline's familiar. Gable like that's not common in Ashmere. Most houses up here are more farmhouse or Dutch colonial."

He glanced up at her. "Where'd you find this?"

"Inside," Isla said, glancing at him wondering what the difference between farmhouse or Dutch colonial style was. "No label. Just hanging on the wall like it's supposed to be forgotten."

Mason looked back at the photo.

"Could be the Croswell place," he said after a second. "But I'm not sure."

Isla filed that away quietly.

"Why're you asking?" he added, not accusatory, just curious.

"I don't know yet," Isla said. "It's just... something about it. And Miranda Voss was inside carrying a box of Meryl's council files like it was nothing."

Mason didn't answer, but she could see the shift in his posture. The way he stilled slightly, like someone stepping off familiar ground.

"You think she took something important?" he asked.

"I think I don't trust people who act helpful too quickly," Isla said. "Especially when the ink's barely dry on someone's obituary."

Mason gave a small nod. "Well... if I hear anything, I'll let you know."

"Thanks."

They lingered half a second longer, not awkward, just *aware*, and then she tucked the phone away.

"You know," Mason said as he started up the steps toward the back entrance, "you're not what I expected when people said you were back in town."

"Hopefully in a good way."

He gave her a sideways smile. "Let you know when I decide."

And then he disappeared inside.

The bell above the door gave its usual half-hearted ring as Isla stepped into Reeve's General Store.

The place smelled faintly of sawdust, old coffee, and cinnamon gum. The floor creaked like it had stories of its own, and the front display, currently featuring a confused arrangement of canned peaches, fishing lures, and allergy tablets, hadn't changed in at least six months.

Isla pondered the connection wondering if someone had come to Amos mentioning an allergy to peaches, fishing, or fishing with peaches.

Behind the counter, Amos Reeve looked up from where he was rearranging a stack of receipts beside a jar of jerky sticks, the age of which concerned Isla.

"Ms. Winters, back again" he said.

"Mr. Reeve," Isla replied.

He didn't ask why she was there. In Ashmere, conversation came free with the groceries.

She approached the counter, eyeing a rack of postcards labeled *3 FOR $1* as if they might offer her a conversation opener. Then she just went with it.

"I wanted to ask you something. About what you said at the diner this morning."

Amos's brow didn't move, but the set of his mouth changed slightly. "Didn't think I said much at all."

"You mentioned Meryl Hartley helped Clarissa Finch during the last election. Something about people asking her."

He picked up the jerky jar and moved it two inches to the left. "She did. Volunteer help. Paperwork. Records. Meryl was always big on details."

"And then?"

102

"She stopped." He didn't look at her, just stared past her at a dusty bag of potting soil. "Didn't say why. Just sort of backed away. Quiet-like."

"Was there a falling out?"

"Not officially. But Clarissa likes her ducks in a row. Meryl wasn't a duck."

Isla folded her arms. "So, what happened?"

"I don't know." He finally looked at her, eyes sharp but not unkind. "But Meryl stopped smiling when she talked about Clarissa. That's usually enough in this town."

A customer walked in behind Isla, glanced around, and left again. The bell gave another tired jingle.

"I'm thinking of talking to Clarissa," Isla said.

"That's your business."

"Is it a bad idea?"

Amos gave a short grunt. "Only if you're expecting a straight answer."

She turned to leave, but he added like a postscript:

"Watch how people react when they think the past is coming back. Tells you everything."

Chapter 13: Clarissa & Cromwell

Clarissa Finch lived rather predictably in a house that looked like it had been staged for a lifestyle magazine called *Executive Small Town*. White porch railings, fresh hydrangeas, and a welcome mat that seemed slightly too clean to be sincere.

Isla barely had time to knock before the door swung open.

"Ms. Winters," Clarissa said, smiling with practiced warmth. "To what do I owe the visit?"

Isla returned the smile. "Hoping for a quick chat. About Meryl Hartley."

Clarissa's expression didn't falter, but her eyes sharpened slightly. "Of course. Come in. Terrible event for the town."

The inside of the house was all controlled charm; bookshelves perfectly spaced, containing books with perfect spines indicating they had never been read. There were three framed photos, a diffuser puffing something floral into the air. Clarissa gestured Isla toward a chair that looked like it might squeak if you weren't polite enough.

"She helped with your last council run," Isla said as they settled. "Didn't she?"

"She did," Clarissa replied, crossing her legs. "Meryl was meticulous, data-driven, principled. She knew how to keep things organized."

"But something changed?" Isla asked.

Clarissa gave a quick, measured shrug. "People grow apart. She became more focused on the Historical Society, and I was... busy moving things forward for Ashmere."

"Any falling out?"

Clarissa's lips tightened just slightly. "Not officially. Though she did grow distant. I chalked it up to differing priorities. Meryl had a strong moral compass, but sometimes it made her... rigid."

Isla nodded, letting that hang.

Then casually, like it had just come to her, she pulled out her phone and swiped to the photo of the unlabeled house.

"Oh, one more thing. Do you know anything about the Croswell Estate? I came across this picture in the museum. Is this it? It just... seems unusual."

Clarissa leaned forward, studying the photo.

"Yes," she said slowly. "That's the old Croswell place, just west of the river bend. It's been abandoned for years."

"No owner?"

"Well, officially it's town land now. At least on paper. The family line got murky. Some distant cousin in Connecticut or California, no one ever claimed it properly. It's one of those places that slipped through the cracks."

She paused.

"A shame, really. Prime land. Could've been something useful."

"Useful?" Isla asked.

Clarissa smiled faintly. "Ashmere has a lot of charm. But charm doesn't pay for infrastructure. I've had a few ideas."

"What ideas?"

"Well, I can tell you that the nearest Walmart is way too far for my liking. Just think, Isla, how much revenue a big store like that would bring for Ashmere."

Isla shuddered at the thought, imagining Ashmere as Walmart Central, its fluorescent lights, chain signage, parking lot sprawl. She thought it best not to debate the merits of *progress* with the councilor.

She tucked her phone away.

"Thanks for your time," she said, rising.

"Of course," Clarissa said, standing with her. "If there's anything I can do to help clear things up, let me know."

Isla stepped onto the porch, the door closing softly behind her.

She walked three steps before letting the breath out of her chest.

She didn't know what Clarissa was hiding if anything.

But that smile had held something Isla recognized.

A future already planned.

And someone in the way.

It took Isla twenty minutes to find the path. It wasn't marked, just a break in the underbrush off a small gravel path past the small fishing jetty. It was a place most people passed without thinking.

The sun hung low behind the trees, painting everything in golds and greens. Birds chirped like nothing had ever gone wrong here. But the air shifted the moment the house came into view.

The Croswell Estate.

What remained of it.

The structure still stood, barely. A once-grand two-story mansion now wrapped in ivy and time. Shingles missing. Porch sagging. The windows stared blankly, glass long since shattered or swallowed by vines. Trees crowded close as if trying to reclaim it.

Isla stepped carefully through the waist-high grass toward the side gate. It gave way with a reluctant groan.

Inside the grounds, the silence thickened.

She made her way toward the house, boots crunching twigs. A porch chair sat tipped on its side like someone had fled mid-sentence. Ferns poked through cracks in the wooden steps.

She climbed them slowly.

The front door was ajar.

Of course it was.

She peeked in, the entry hall barely visible through the gloom. Wallpaper peeling in long, theatrical strips. Floor warped in waves.

She didn't go inside. Not yet.

Instead, she circled to the side of the house, past a cracked sundial and a row of overgrown hedges. That's when it happened.

A *crack* sudden, sharp. and then a *thud* just feet from where she stood.

Isla jumped, heart hammering. A small, moss-covered statue, maybe once a cherub, now just an eroded face and broken wing had tipped off its crumbling pedestal and landed in the grass beside her.

She stared at it.

"Not cool," she muttered aloud, catching her breath.

She crouched down, brushing the dirt away. The statue's base had been cracked for years. Age, not intention.

Still.

She looked back toward the house.

Something about the way it loomed; *silent, waiting*, gave her goosebumps.

She didn't go in. Not today.

But she stayed a moment longer, just watching. Not searching. Just trying to understand what kind of place kept standing long after everyone had left.

Then she turned and made her way back down the path.

Behind her, the Croswell house stayed still.

But not empty.

Chapter 14: Dusty Clues

The museum air still smelled faintly of lemon polish and dust, an odd combination of cleaning and neglecting. Isla stepped inside without fanfare, the bell above the door giving its usual dry, judgmental click.

No one was at the front desk.

Again.

She let the silence settle around her like a shawl, cool and familiar. The morning light filtered through the high windows in golden shafts, catching motes of dust that hadn't yet decided whether to rise or fall. It made everything look suspended, like the room hadn't taken a breath since Meryl was last in it.

She walked quietly toward the back office.

A polite sign still hung crookedly on the half-open door: "Staff Only – Please Knock (but gently)." Isla ignored it and slipped inside.

Meryl's office wasn't large. It was more of a nook attached to the main room, but it had the layered feeling of someone who lived through paper. Neat but dense. Not messy. Intentional clutter.

A thin layer of dust had started to gather on the keyboard and desk lamp. But the rest looked untouched. Isla's eyes moved over the carefully labeled folders on the shelves: *Ashmere Rail Line (1887–1901)*, *Flood Recovery Records*, *Private Collections (Unsorted)*.

Sticky notes fluttered lightly at the edges of documents. Some were coded with shorthand. Others just had quiet reminders written in Meryl's sharp, deliberate handwriting:

"Follow up with town clerk?"
"Clarissa request = pending re-check ordinance 19B."
"Croswell see safe file"

Isla frowned at that last one.

She moved to the filing cabinet beneath the desk and pulled open the bottom drawer, more out of instinct than anything. It gave a reluctant groan; not locked, just stubborn. Inside: manila folders, most labelled, one torn at the edge and slightly askew. No tab. No title.

She eased it out, the edges brittle with age but the contents newer, as if the folder had been reused many times. Tucked in the middle was a crisp sheet, folded once, and a torn envelope marked in thick black pen: *CROSWELL INHERITANCE – URGENT*

Isla unfolded the paper carefully.

It wasn't official town letterhead. But it *looked* real enough. A draft development application showing a proposed zoning change for the Croswell estate area, with several penciled notes in the margins. There were outlines for a multi-lot retail plan, including:

Big Box Anchor Tenant (preliminary: Walmart)

Parking Extension (100+ spaces)

Phased residential development (Phase 3 – TBD)

And at the bottom a half-scanned signature:

Clarissa Finch
Ashmere Town Council (Zoning Subcom.)

Isla's brow furrowed.

She checked the back. No date. No stamp. No clear approval trail. But it didn't look like a draft. It looked like something that was already being prepared.

Her fingers traced the edge of the torn envelope. Half the flap was gone, ripped hastily.

Something about it felt off. Too clean. Too quiet.

Why was this in Meryl's drawer?

Why wasn't it labeled? Why would the envelope say inheritance but it contains council documents?

And why hide it in a file with no tab?

She looked again at the sticky note on the wall behind the desk.

Croswell. See safe file

There was no safe in sight.

But there was a small key taped to the underside of the desk drawer, barely visible, as if someone thought no one would ever bother to check.

Isla pocketed it.

She slipped the development paper back into the torn folder but not before snapping a photo with her phone. Just in case.

Then she carefully slid the drawer shut and stepped back from the desk.

A floorboard creaked behind her.

Isla froze, heart catching for just a moment. But when she turned, no one was there. Just the building settling. Or remembering.

She exhaled.

Then quietly made her way out, not bothering to close the office door behind her.

Because someone else would notice eventually.

And maybe that's what she wanted.

Chapter 15: Ashes and Flowers

Isla knew something was off the moment she turned the corner onto Main and saw the scorched wood.

The museum's front porch, once a tired but dependable shade of green-grey, now bore a jagged scar along its left corner, blackened boards curling inward like dried leaves. Smoke stains crept up the siding above the railing. One of the front windows had cracked down the middle, held together only by grime and the stubbornness of old glass.

She stopped just outside the museum gate.

The smell still lingered, charcoal. Not overpowering, but unmistakable. Like the end of a campfire someone had tried to pretend never happened.

A figure moved near the porch steps, crouched low beside a pile of half-splintered planks and damp ash.

"Mason?"

He looked up, sleeves rolled to his elbows, a screwdriver tucked in his pocket and a pencil behind his ear, like he couldn't decide what the job actually was.

"Oh hey," he said, standing and brushing ash from his jeans. "I didn't think they'd let anyone near this yet."

"Don't worry. I'm here in an unofficial capacity. Just...
nosy."

Mason gave a small half-smile. "Good. Then I don't
have to explain why I'm fixing things I wasn't asked to
touch."

She stepped closer, eyes scanning the damage. "Is this
what it looks like?"

"Yep. Fire. Small one. Started sometime after midnight, I
was told". He gestured to the scorched boards near the
window. "Ronny said it was likely deliberate."

Isla raised an eyebrow. "Ronny used the word
'deliberate'?"

"Well. He actually said 'some shady fire starter did a bad
job.' But I translated."

She knelt beside the base of the porch, fingertips
brushing lightly against the soot-blackened wood. Some
of the boards were newer now, already replaced, but
others were just scorched, brittle at the edges.

"What did they use?"

"Could've been a gas accelerant. Could've been lighter
fluid. No smell now, but Ronny said the FD found
scorch patterns that didn't match a candle or electrical
short."

Isla looked up at the museum's front windows. One
curtain was gone completely; the other hung limply,
greyed by smoke.

Then her eyes narrowed.

The photo wall.

Visible through the main window. the wall of town photos that had drawn her in the first time. Rows of black-and-white portraits, group shots, and dusty glimpses of Ashmere's past. All intact.

She leaned closer to the museum window, squinting through soot-smeared glass. One frame hung at an angle, the glass spiderwebbed with cracks. And the photo of the Croswell estate?

Edges curled inward. The corner nearest the edge charred to ash. Not gone. But almost.

Mason joined her, following her gaze.

"Photo wall mostly made it," he said. "Lucky break, huh?"

"Maybe," Isla said quietly.

He didn't press.

They both turned as the museum door creaked open from the inside. A faint gust of burnt air escaped. Miranda Voss stepped out, one gloved hand braced against the doorframe, the other smoothing down a perfectly pressed coat that hadn't seen smoke in its life.

"Isla," she said, with a practiced breath of surprise. "Mason."

"Museum's still standing," Mason said, neutral.

"Barely," Miranda replied. "I just stopped in to check on the archive cabinet. Some of Meryl's files were due to be transferred next week."

"Lucky they weren't already moved," Isla said, watching her face.

Miranda smiled. Just enough.

She stepped down onto the porch carefully, as if the ash might stain her intentions. Her boots were clean. Too clean.

"I spoke with Deputy Patch earlier," she said. "He seemed... flustered."

"Probably because someone tried to burn down a building and he had to remember his training manual."

Miranda gave a soft, approving laugh. "Yes, well. He said it appeared to be arson, but likely just vandalism. Some local boys with too much beer and too few hobbies."

"Did Ronny say that?" Isla asked. "Or did you?"

Miranda's smile didn't waver. "I'm just repeating what I was told."

She glanced back at the door. "Still, it's unsettling. I hadn't been here in... well, a few days. And now this."

Mason raised an eyebrow. "You weren't here yesterday? Afternoon?" Isla asked.

"No," Miranda said smoothly. "I was at the council building, helping Clarissa prep some of the economic development materials for her presentation next week. Why?"

"Just curious," Isla said, watching the way Miranda's gloved hand tightened slightly around the strap of her tote.

"Well," Miranda said, as if closing an internal tab. "Let's hope whoever did this is caught. Meryl may have been... particular, even peculiar, but she took pride in preserving Ashmere's history. This building mattered to her."

She turned to Isla. "I trust you're not planning to dig too deeply into this?"

"Into what?"

Miranda's voice lowered just a touch. "The fire. The files. Meryl's affairs. I'd hate to see your return to town become complicated. People are grieving. And gossip... doesn't help."

Isla gave her a small, dry smile. "Well, I'm not gossiping. I'm just looking at what's burnt and what isn't."

Miranda held the eye contact just a second longer than polite. Then she turned, descending the rest of the porch steps and gliding toward the sidewalk like someone leaving a negotiation.

Once she was out of earshot, Isla murmured, "Do you think she practiced that speech in her bathroom mirror?"

Mason chuckled softly. "Three times. With lighting."

Isla stared back at the photo wall through the glass.

Nothing damaged. Nothing missing.

Nothing accidental.

The flower shop smelled like rainwater and rosemary.

Tessa always said she preferred fresh herbs to artificial sweetness. The result was a space that felt less like a retail business and more like a warm greenhouse that occasionally agreed to sell things.

Buckets of blooms stood in half-circles near the windows. There were peonies, tulips, wildflowers for customers who "just wanted pink." The floor creaked gently as Isla stepped inside.

Tessa emerged from the back, arms full of eucalyptus stems.

"Oh good," she said, without preamble. "I was hoping it was you and not another person asking if we deliver to people allergic to pollen."

Isla gave a small grin. "Is that a common problem?"

"Twice a week, minimum. One guy wanted a 'non-threatening bouquet.' I offered him a rock."

Isla wandered toward the counter, trailing a hand across a row of mismatched vases. "This place looks the same."

"Because I don't change things," Tessa replied. "That's my secret. Also: laziness."

She deposited the eucalyptus into a wide metal bucket, wiping her hands on her apron. Then she turned, eyes narrowing just a little.

"So," she said. "You're really going around asking people about Meryl Hartley?"

Isla paused.

It wasn't accusatory. But it wasn't not, either.

"I'm not interrogating anyone," she said. "Just... talking."

Tessa crossed her arms loosely, leaning back against the wall. "Talking about a woman who died under strange circumstances. And asking the kind of questions that make people uncomfortable."

Isla gave her a look. "Do *you* feel uncomfortable?"

"No," Tessa said, then hesitated. "But I feel... cautious. This town doesn't like being examined too closely. You know that."

"I'm not trying to unravel Ashmere," Isla said. "Just figure out why no one else seems to care that something about Meryl's death feels... wrong."

Tessa studied her. "You always did have a weird relationship with 'wrong.'"

"I don't even know what I'm looking for yet," Isla admitted. "It's not about closure. I'm not some trauma tourist. I just…"

She trailed off, unsure how to phrase it.

Tessa filled the silence gently. "It's curiosity, isn't it?"

Isla looked up.

Tessa smiled, softer now. "You always were a curious one. You used to chase frogs down to the river just to see what they were hiding."

"They were *hiding frogs,* Tessa. It was not that mysterious."

Tessa laughed. "You once climbed onto the school roof because someone told you there was a message carved into the chimney."

"Okay, that one was legitimate," Isla said. "It said 'Ashmere eats its own.'"

Tessa raised her eyebrows. "Which you decided was either a punk rock lyric... or a prophecy."

"Well. Jury's still out."

They both chuckled, the sound light, genuine.

Tessa walked over to the register, fiddling with a small roll of twine she didn't really need to fix. "I just don't want to see you get tangled in something no one's willing to help you untangle."

"I'm already tangled," Isla said. "I found a document. Zoning stuff. Clarissa's signature. Tied to the Croswell estate."

Tessa blinked. "That old place? I thought it was just... nature's storage unit now."

"Apparently not. Meryl had the file. Hidden. And now the museum's been partially burnt."

Tessa's face shifted. Concern, surprise, something else.

"Do you think... that's connected?"

"I think Meryl was onto something. And I think she got silenced for it."

Silence stretched between them, not awkward, just uncertain.

Tessa exhaled. "You're going to keep pulling at this, aren't you?"

"I don't know how not to," Isla said.

Tessa nodded slowly, the corner of her mouth lifting. "Well, in that case... come with me."

She led Isla to the back, past a curtain strung up with old postcards and dried lavender. A tiny break room sat behind it. A small fridge, chipped glass, a faded corkboard covered in coupons and bad puns.

Tessa reached into a drawer and pulled out a tin of cookies.

"Support provisions," she said. "Hazelnut. Stolen from my aunt's pantry."

Isla took one, grinning. "This is how you lure me into emotional vulnerability, isn't it?"

"No," Tessa said. "That's what the tea is for."

They sat quietly for a while. Just two women. One with dirt under her nails. One with too many questions.

Outside, a truck passed slowly on the street. Wind jostled the doorframe. The shop returned to its hum.

"I missed this," Isla said finally.

"The flowers?"

"No. The part where someone lets me talk without needing a point."

Tessa nodded. "That's what friends are for. And hazelnut cookies."

Chapter 16: Hank & Miranda

The trail behind town was quieter than usual.

Isla followed the path as it curved past the old water tower and dipped into the woods towards Hank's place. It smelled like pine needles and morning fog, the kind of clean that made everything else feel suspicious by comparison.

Hank Delaney's cottage sat tucked in a fold of trees like it had been placed there by nature, not design. The porch sagged slightly in the middle. Wind chimes made from old spoons clinked softly, as if even they weren't in the mood to make noise.

She knocked once against the porch railing.

Then a voice from inside: "It's open."

She stepped in.

The door creaked but didn't resist. Inside smelled like cedar, tobacco, and something vaguely medicinal. Hank sat near the fireplace, legs crossed, hands on his knees, except they weren't resting. They were twitching slightly, fingers brushing against his pant leg like they had something to say.

"Hank," she greeted. "Hope I'm not interrupting."

He looked up slowly, eyes clear but unreadable.

"You usually are," he said. "But you're polite about it."

She gave a dry smile and nodded toward the hearth. "Fire going this early in the day?"

"Just burned off some damp. Helps with the cold in the floorboards."

She stepped closer, glancing toward the stone-ringed fire pit in the center of the room. The flames had burned down to a soft orange glow, but something inside caught her eye.

Not a log. Not paper.

A half-melted strip of plastic, edges warped, faint lettering scorched beyond recognition. It didn't look like it belonged to any firewood bundle.

"You always throw recyclables in with the kindling?" she asked, casual.

Hank didn't look. "Just old junk. Stuff that doesn't matter anymore."

She didn't press.

Not yet.

Instead, she pulled up the stool across from him and sat, elbows on knees. "I saw the museum this morning."

He didn't react.

"Fire did some damage," she added. "Mostly the porch, but... someone definitely wanted to send a message. Or erase one."

Still no reaction. Just a slow blink.

"Funny thing," she said, letting the words stretch. "One of the museum windows cracked from the heat. But the Croswell photo wall inside? Still standing. Almost untouched."

That got him.

Not a flinch. But his hands stopped moving.

Isla let the silence settle, then asked lightly, "You haven't been down that way recently, have you?"

Hank looked at her. Really looked.

"I go where I go," he said.

She nodded toward his hands. "You always get soot on your knuckles cleaning out the fireplace?"

He shifted in his chair.

"Stacked some wood wrong," he said. "Had to reach in to fix it."

She didn't answer.

Just looked at him.

The kind of look that said, *you've raised raccoons with more convincing alibis.*

Hank sighed, not frustrated, not angry. Just... tired.

"I didn't set a fire at the museum," he said. "And you didn't come here expecting me to confess anything."

"True," Isla said. "But I did wonder if you'd look me in the eye when you said it."

He did.

And that was the strangest part; he didn't look like a liar. He looked like a man who *knew something* and didn't know what to do with it.

Or worse, someone who thought it wouldn't matter if he kept it to himself.

Hank stood, slowly, and moved toward the small counter near the kitchen. He poured himself a cup of black coffee from a thermos and didn't offer one to her.

"You poke too much, Winters," he said. "This towns not built to be poked."

Isla stood, brushing her hands on her jeans. "Neither was a fire pit, but here we are."

She stepped toward the door, pausing only once to glance back at the fireplace. The plastic had burned deeper now. Almost gone. Whatever it had been, it wasn't meant to last.

"Be careful with your burn pile," she said as she opened the door. "Sometimes things flare up bigger than you meant."

Hank didn't reply.

He just sat back down and watched the fire like it owed him something.

The knock came just after eleven.

Three quick, polite taps: not loud, not uncertain. The kind of knock that assumed permission would follow.

Isla glanced at the half-swept floor, then at her hoodie slung over the back of a kitchen chair, then at the general state of her life. "Great," she muttered. "Let me just tidy the existential chaos."

She opened the door.

Miranda Voss stood on the porch, perfectly centered, holding a cream-colored folder and wearing a soft smile that didn't reach her eyes.

"Good morning," she said.

Isla leaned against the doorframe. "Can I help you?"

Miranda's eyes flicked past her, taking in the cottage interior. "I hope I'm not interrupting anything important."

"Just my deep meditation with instant coffee."

Miranda stepped inside without waiting.

Isla followed, letting the screen door creak closed behind her. She resisted the urge to kick the scatter rug into alignment.

"Spartan," Miranda said, looking around. "Functional. Honest."

"Thanks," Isla said. "I'll get that framed."

Miranda set the folder down on the kitchen counter and adjusted the sleeve of her jacket. "I was on my way to the community center. Thought I might stop in. I've been hearing your name around town."

Isla crossed her arms. "Well, we all need a hobby."

Miranda turned slightly, hands clasped. "You've been asking questions still like before. Visiting the museum. Speaking with Hank. Rumor has it you even cornered poor Amos Reeve."

"He cornered *me*. With monologues about drone toothpaste."

Miranda gave a smile that could have been cut from parchment. "Isla... I understand that you're curious. But I'd caution against stirring up more unrest. People are grieving. The town needs stability, not suspicion."

Isla tilted her head. "Didn't realize curiosity was on the banned list."

"Of course not," Miranda said smoothly. "But there's a difference between remembrance and re-opening wounds. Meryl's death was unfortunate. No one wants to see it politicized."

Isla's eyebrows lifted. "I never mentioned politics."

There was a pause. Just long enough.

Miranda's smile slipped by half a millimeter, like a hairline crack in porcelain.

"Well," she said, recovering quickly. "It's a small town. Everything becomes politics eventually."

Isla let that hang.

Miranda picked up the folder again, tapping the corner lightly against her palm. "We're preparing some memorial materials for the upcoming newsletter. A community remembrance. I thought perhaps you might like to contribute something. A memory. A quote. Even a photograph, if you had one."

"I didn't know Meryl well when I was younger," Isla said.

Miranda nodded. "Sometimes not knowing someone is the clearest view."

That sounded like it meant something, but not in a way Isla was ready to unpack.

Miranda moved toward the bookshelf; a small, lopsided thing holding mismatched novels and old guidebooks. Her fingers hovered near the spines but didn't touch.

"It's strange," she said lightly. "The Croswell estate came up recently. Clarissa mentioned it during our meeting she said you were asking about it."

Isla blinked.

"I must've left a bigger impression than I thought," Isla said.

Miranda glanced back, smile returning. "Well, Clarissa has a good memory for things that matter."

Too smooth.

Too early.

She'd slipped.

Isla said nothing, just walked to the counter and casually opened a drawer, as if looking for something that wasn't there.

Miranda set the folder down again. "I should be going. But I do hope you'll consider writing something for the remembrance issue. We want to capture the heart of Ashmere, not just its history."

Isla followed her to the door.

"Let me guess," she said. "Deadline's tight?"

Miranda's eyes twinkled, almost amused. "Aren't they always?"

She stepped onto the porch, pausing to adjust her scarf. "And Isla… just as a suggestion… if you're going to keep digging into Ashmere's past, try not to get so caught up in it that you forget the present."

"I'll try," Isla said. "But it's hard not to notice when the past keeps catching fire."

Miranda's smile didn't waver.

But she walked a little faster down the driveway than she had up.

When she was gone, Isla leaned against the doorframe and exhaled.

Clarissa mentioned it.

She stared at the folder on the counter, still unopened, then at the floor, where ash from the museum still clung to the soles of her boots.

Why does she care what I ask?

Unless I'm getting too close.

Unless Meryl already did.

Ashmere's cemetery was tucked behind a low stone wall, just past the bend in the old orchard road. No gate, no signage. Just a wooden post with a weathered placard that read:

In Memory. Not in Marble.

The sky had the decency to stay grey.

About thirty people stood scattered across the lawn, their umbrellas forming a loose patchwork of navy, floral, and the occasional half-broken CVS special umbrella. No choir. No speeches beyond the pastor's soft reading. Just wind, wet grass, and the quiet shuffle of feet trying not to sink into the mud.

Isla stood near the back.

She hadn't known Meryl Hartley well. Not really. But she felt something tugging at her spine. Not grief. Not yet. Something closer to obligation. To witness.

Clarissa Finch dabbed at her eyes with a tissue. It was crisp, white, and far too clean to have seen much use. Her crying came in measured intervals. As if they were brief bursts of theatrical sorrow, followed by recovery that felt a bit too practiced.

Isla didn't blame her. People grieve however they can. Some felt the need for performance.

But she watched all the same.

Amos Reeve stood off to the side, hands in his coat pockets, gaze not on the casket but on the trees behind it. He looked like a man attending a weather report, not a funeral. No hat. No umbrella. Just static.

Hank Delaney didn't show.

No surprise there. Not after their conversation.

Mason Wilder caught Isla's eye across the fold of mourners and gave her a subtle nod. Not a smile. Just a quiet look that said, *you're not the only one who thinks this doesn't feel right.*

The pastor wrapped up with a prayer that barely rose above the wind. A few people shifted, uncomfortable. Not because of the cold but because of the silence. It was the kind that didn't end neatly.

Then, from just beside Isla, a voice, low, aged, and clear:

"Meryl was asking questions again."

Isla turned slightly. A small woman in a plum coat stood beside her, back slightly hunched, but eyes sharp behind thick glasses.

"About things no one asks about anymore," the woman added.

"Sorry?" Isla said.

The woman blinked, as if surprised she'd spoken aloud.

"Oh, nothing," she said. "Just... she used to come by the archives, years back. Always digging through old zoning maps. Council meeting minutes from when I was a child, if you can believe it."

She paused.

"Last I heard, she was trying to find out why the Croswell estate deed was marked as 'temporary custodial holding.'"

Isla's breath caught.

"That mean something to you?" the woman asked.

"Possibly," Isla said. "Thank you."

The woman nodded and turned her attention back to the casket, murmuring something like a prayer under her breath.

As the service ended, mourners began to drift in clusters. Some polite hugs, brief conversations, the occasional casserole plan. A man near the front, one of the town maintenance workers, said softly to someone Isla couldn't see:

"Poor Meryl. She really thought she was going to change things."

It wasn't mocking. It was resigned.

Clarissa passed Isla on her way out, dabbing once more at her still-dry eyes. She gave Isla a soft, solemn smile that seemed like it belonged on a magazine cover.

"Are you writing something about her?" Clarissa asked, almost sweetly.

Isla blinked. "Why would I be?"

"Oh, just a rumor," Clarissa said. "I'd be happy to proof it. I knew Meryl quite well, despite... differences. We all want to remember her properly."

She walked off before Isla could reply.

Of course she did.

Mason came up beside her a moment later.

"Didn't seem like a lot of grief," he said, quietly.

"Felt more like an apology that no one wanted to make out loud," Isla said.

They stood in silence for a few moments, watching the final shovelfuls of earth fall.

"She was asking questions," Isla said.

"She always was," Mason replied. "That's what made her impossible. And valuable."

Isla nodded.

Then, almost to herself, she whispered, "And now I am too."

Mason gave her a sideways glance. "Careful. That kind of role gets you invited to funerals."

Isla smiled faintly. "Better that than forgetting why they matter."

As the last of the townsfolk made their way toward the cars, Isla lingered a moment longer, hands in her coat pockets.

The Croswell estate. The museum. A file marked urgent. A photo almost burned. And now, a funeral filled with people who mourned with silence more than sorrow.

Something had happened.

And someone still wanted it buried.

Chapter 17: Books

Riverbend Books smelled like and lemon balm tea and lavender.

Isla stepped inside pushing the door with some effort, its hinges clearly old with fatigue. It wasn't so much a shop as a reading cave with cash register privileges. A collection of mismatched armchairs, crooked lamps, and book piles that defied structural logic complete with the many random paper tags with handwriting on them.

She made her way to the back corner table without asking. The clerk this time was a sharp-eyed woman named Marla with a bun like a warning sign. As Isla passed, she nodded once from behind the counter and returned to her knitting.

The table's surface was uneven, warped from years of forgotten mugs, but perfect for what Isla needed: space to think. Without fear of a raccoon ambush.

She pulled out the folded development document. The one from Meryl's drawer, still smelling faintly of polish and old secrets, and laid it flat. The Walmart plans. The zoning changes. The penciled notes. Clarissa Finch's half-scanned signature.

It still didn't make sense.

Why hide a zoning plan in a folder labeled *inheritance*?

Why keep it unfiled, buried under other folders?

She reached into her bag and pulled out a slim, worn copy of *Ashmere: A Historical Survey*. It was the kind of book every town had. Part memory, part myth, mostly photocopies. She skimmed the index.

Croswell Estate – 188, 213-214, 238–240

She flipped.

Page 213 had a grainy photo of the estate in its heyday. Tall windows, curved staircases, ivy like veins over stone. But page 214 was different.

A single paragraph, then a gap.

As if something had been removed, and the formatting hadn't quite recovered.

She held the book up to the light. No sign of a torn page. No glue remnants. Just... absence.

On the bottom of the page was a small italic note: *See town deed records, Archive Ref. 1957–CRO.*

She pulled out her notebook, jotting it down.

From the front of the shop, Marla's voice floated over.

"If you're trying to disappear into a conspiracy, at least buy the book afterward."

Isla looked up. "You know me. Frugal detective work."

Marla crossed her arms. "Meryl used to sit right there, you know. That exact table. Brought in her own folders. Spilled tea on the carpet once saying it added character."

"Did she say what she was looking for?"

"Said she was chasing ghosts," Marla replied. "I told her I stock plenty of those in the fiction section."

"Did she take anything?"

Marla tilted her head toward the local history shelf. "Only book missing is *Ashmere Property Transitions 1900–1980*. We don't even really lend. But Meryl, well she as known well to us."

Isla walked over and scanned the shelf. Sure enough, a thin gap between volumes. Enough for a slender binder or town-issued reference.

She stared at it for a moment, fingers resting on the empty space like it might confess something.

Back at the table, she unfolded the zoning document again. At the bottom, just above Clarissa's signature, were three faintly visible digits in the margin:

Ref: 1957-CRO

Same as the archive code from the history book.

So, Meryl was cross-referencing.

And she'd found something she wasn't meant to.

Isla looked up at Marla again. "Was Meryl here last week?"

"Tuesday, I think," Marla said. "She looked... frustrated. Said she thought the town had forgotten on purpose. Like remembering was the most dangerous thing you could do."

"That's unusually poetic for zoning law."

Marla shrugged. "She was in deep. I asked if she was writing a book. She said no. Said she was trying to stop one."

That sat with Isla for a long moment.

She packed the papers away gently, slid the history book under her arm, and walked to the counter.

"I'll buy it," she said. "Consider it a donation to your ghost fund."

Marla smirked. "Try not to get haunted."

Isla stepped back into the grey afternoon light with a deeper chill than before.

Ref. 1957–CRO.
A missing property book.
A file labeled *inheritance*.
And a woman chasing ghosts.

It wasn't just about what Meryl found.

It was about who wanted her to stop.

Chapter 18: Amos & Raccoon

The general store smelled like cedar chips and cinnamon gum, the kind of scent that stuck to the back of your throat, like time.

It was nearly closing. The last customer left with a bag of peanut brittle and a goodbye.

Isla stood near the counter, browsing a display of overly enthusiastic dish towels. One read: *I don't need therapy, I have coffee.*

She wasn't convinced.

Amos Reeve was sweeping near the back. His posture, normally a mix of proud and grumbly, was subdued, like someone walking through a memory.

"You need anything, Miss Winters?" he called without looking up.

"Just trying to decide if these towels are ironic or tragic," she replied.

He didn't laugh. He didn't even grunt. Just rested the broom against the wall and wiped his hands on his apron.

Then he walked over slowly, glancing toward the door as if checking for witnesses. None.

"I need to tell you something," he said. "Just quietly."

Isla straightened. "Alright."

He scratched the side of his nose, eyes flicking once toward the old radio on the shelf, still playing a warbly tune from the '60s.

"Meryl came to me," he said. "Week before the festival. Asked if I still had those old zoning maps from the '80s. The ones the council 'misplaced' when they digitized the archives."

"You had them?" Isla asked.

He nodded. "I keep everything. Some call it hoarding. I call it municipal paranoia."

"Did you give them to her?"

"Course I did. Told her they were in rough shape, and the coffee stain wasn't a metaphor."

"What did she say?"

Amos hesitated.

"Said she was going to blow the whole thing open," he murmured. "Said the land wasn't theirs to sell. That the Croswell deed had been handled... improperly. Quietly. Years ago."

He rubbed the back of his neck, then leaned on the counter like it had answers.

"I thought she was spinning her wheels," he admitted. "Meryl always had a cause. Always thought the town needed protecting, usually from itself."

Isla let the silence stretch, but he wasn't done.

"I didn't take her seriously," he said, voice low. "Told her maybe let sleeping land lie."

"And now?" Isla asked.

Amos didn't look at her. He stared at the sugar display, as if debating the moral weight of caramel.

"Now I think maybe that land wasn't sleeping. Just waiting."

He exhaled through his nose. "I keep thinking if I'd said more, warned someone... maybe..."

"You did what you thought was right," Isla said. "You helped her. That counts."

"Only if the truth survives," he muttered.

He picked up the broom again, like the conversation had never happened.

Isla watched him for a moment, then turned toward the exit.

"Thanks, Amos," she said softly.

He didn't reply.

Back at her cottage the window stuck again.

Isla muttered something unprintable and jammed the handle upward with a little more spite than necessary. It gave an unpleasant creak, like it was morally opposed to fresh air.

She'd finally caved and decided to clean the front windows of the cottage. Mostly because the layer of grime had reached a point where even denial couldn't pretend it was ambiance.

She grabbed the vinegar spray and gave it a half-hearted spritz, then wiped in slow circles, wondering if anyone had ever actually died of mild resentment.

The sun shifted behind the clouds, casting a shadow across the glass.

Isla blinked.

Then stepped back.

There, perched like a mildly furious gargoyle on the window ledge outside, was the raccoon.

The same one. She knew it. It had the same permanent scowl, the same cocked head like it was evaluating her credit score. Which, let's face it, after years in New York City was not the best.

It stared at her.

She stared back.

"Don't even think about it," she said, wiping another circle just to maintain moral superiority.

The raccoon narrowed its eyes. Its tail twitched once.

Then it lunged.

Or tried to.

It slipped slightly on the mossy edge of the window frame and *thudded* against the glass with an undignified squeak. Claws scrabbled. Nose smushed. For one glorious second, it looked like a disgruntled pancake.

Isla didn't move.

She just stared, cloth still in hand, and said flatly:

"I'm sorry. Were you trying to assassinate me or just critique my technique?"

The raccoon hissed, recoiled, then, with great drama, vanished off the sill, leaving only a smudge and the faint insult of a retreating tail.

Isla stared at the pawprints.

Then sighed.

"Well," she muttered, "at least someone's keeping an eye on me."

She sprayed the glass again and went back to wiping.

Only now, she added one more item to her mental list of enemies:

1. Whoever buried the Croswell estate paperwork
2. Whoever lit the fire
3. Clarissa Finch
4. And one vindictive raccoon with boundary issues

Chapter 19: Clarissa & The Safe

Ashmere Town Hall always looked outdated even for a small town like this. The lobby was dim, lined with faded photos of past mayors and a sad Ficus that had been slowly dying since 2008. A poster near the elevator advertised *"Community Budget Listening Night"* in Comic Sans.

Isla stepped up to the reception desk and gave the teenager behind it her best polite smile.

"I'm here to see Clarissa Finch," she said.

The girl checked a clipboard that definitely wasn't necessary, then waved vaguely toward the hallway.

"Second office on the left."

Clarissa's door was half-open. She was inside, typing something with the intensity of a novelist on deadline, though Isla was fairly certain it was just an email about parking permits.

"Clarissa," Isla said.

Clarissa glanced up, startled, then arranged her features into a diplomatic smile. "Miss Winters. I wasn't expecting you."

"Not many people do," Isla said, stepping in and closing the door behind her.

Clarissa's smile didn't falter, but her hands paused above the keyboard. "What can I help you with?"

Isla stayed standing. "I came across a zoning document. Rough draft. Walmart, parking lot, the works."

Clarissa leaned back slightly. "Ah. That."

"You know it?"

"We had various versions over the years. Nothing that ever made it past early discussion. It's common practice to model hypothetical development scenarios, especially for grant projections."

"Funny," Isla said. "It had your signature."

Clarissa shrugged. "Templates get reused. Sometimes people sign off to acknowledge receipt, not approval. I won't deny I wanted Ashmere to move with the times, I told you that."

"It was in Meryl's office. Hidden."

That earned a flicker. Small, fast. The blink of a woman who'd stepped on a rake.

Clarissa recovered. "I'm not sure why Meryl would've had that. She wasn't on any active committees."

"She was looking into the Croswell estate," Isla said. "Seems she found something."

Clarissa smoothed a folder on her desk that didn't need smoothing. "The Croswell property has been in a holding pattern for years. It's deteriorating. That's not sustainable."

"Is that why the zoning file was marked *urgent?*"

Clarissa's lips twitched. "Zoning requests are often time-sensitive."

"Especially when the original deed's status is unclear?"

Now Clarissa's smile thinned.

"I'm not sure what you're implying," she said.

"I'm not implying," Isla said. "I'm asking."

Clarissa stood and walked to the window behind her desk, back straight, hands folded. "Ashmere is struggling. People don't want to admit it, but we are. Infrastructure costs. Housing stagnation. We're ten years behind neighboring towns."

"And a big box store solves that?"

"It brings revenue."

"It buries history."

Clarissa turned. "History doesn't pay for school roofs, Miss Winters."

There it was. The voice of the campaign flyer: practical, polished, and just sharp enough to cut.

Isla took a breath.

"There's something else," Clarissa said, tone softening. "You should be careful. The town's small. People talk. And if you go digging too hard, people start wondering what you're trying to prove."

Isla raised an eyebrow. "Funny. That's what Miranda said. Almost word for word."

Clarissa's eyes flicked. Just a second. Then reset.

"Miranda's... protective. Of Ashmere. Of the council."

"She's protective of something."

There was a pause.

Then Clarissa said, *"Whatever she had in that safe file probably wasn't even relevant."*

Isla blinked. *"I'm sorry what file?"*

Clarissa stilled. Just for a breath. Just enough.

"I mean... she labeled everything," Clarissa said, recovering. "You know Meryl. I'm just assuming that's what you're digging through. You know, all those folders, old files..."

"I never mentioned anything about a file."

Clarissa smiled, but it didn't quite reach her eyes. "Didn't you? Huh. Maybe someone else did. The museum's been all anyone talks about lately."

"Right."

Isla let the silence work for a second, then stepped back toward the door.

"One last thing," she said.

Clarissa looked up, that cool political smile snapping back into place.

"If I go digging," Isla said, "it won't be to prove something. It'll be to remember what mattered. Even if Ashmere forgot."

Clarissa didn't reply.

But her hand gripped the edge of her desk like it wanted to disappear into the woodgrain.

It was nearly dusk when Isla let herself back into the museum.

Shadows stretched long across the parquet floor, and the silence was thick enough to trip on.

She didn't bother turning on the lights. They cast too many questions.

Instead, she moved quietly past the old exhibits. A rusted weathervane, a newspaper clipping about Ashmere's first post office, a mannequin dressed as a 1910 milkmaid who looked like she regretted every life decision.

Straight to Meryl's office.

The door creaked open like it, too, was reluctant to revisit whatever Meryl had tucked away. Isla crouched beside the desk, reached underneath, and pulled free the small key she'd kept inside the lining of her jacket.

Showtime.

She tried the key in every drawer, just to be sure. Nothing.

Then her eyes landed on the filing cabinet. Not the one under the desk, but the old steel one tucked into the side nook that had escaped her attention last time. She hadn't checked that yet. It looked harmless, Bureaucratic. Slightly dented, like someone had once kicked it for misfiling a grant.

She tried the key in the bottom drawer.

It clicked.

Of course it did.

Inside was a false bottom. Noting elegant, just a lifted tray. Isla tugged at the lip until it gave way with a reluctant *thunk*, revealing a shallow steel cavity no bigger than a shoebox.

At the back: a black envelope, sealed with a faded sticker that read:

CROSWELL : HOLDING STATUS: 1979

Isla stared.

Then slowly, carefully, lifted it out.

Inside was a single legal-sized page, folded twice. Thick paper. Real ink. The kind that ghosts stain.

She opened it.

Ashmere Council Memorandum, Internal
Date: March 12, 1979
Subject: Estate Transfer of Croswell Holding Trust

Per the 1974 emergency acquisition and interim custodial agreement, the Croswell estate is to remain under municipal trust until formal heir designation is resolved. No development, zoning action, or transfer may proceed without judicial review and signature approval from the original Croswell line or designated legal substitute.

This designation is filed under Council Ref. 79-CHT and shall be maintained in perpetuity until override or public release.

Signed:
Gerald D. Hutchins
Ashmere Legal Affairs, 1979

Isla sat back slowly, the room quiet except for the hum of her pulse.

Trust. Not owned. Not zoned.

Held.

Which meant every plan Clarissa had signed, every redevelopment draft, every quietly penciled Walmart, was not just controversial.

It was illegal.

She flipped the memo over. No copies attached. But there, scrawled in Meryl's unmistakable handwriting:

"Find the original ref file. This is the stopgap."

So, this wasn't even the full record.

But it was enough.

Enough to prove that Meryl had found it. Enough to explain why she'd hidden it. Enough to make someone nervous.

Isla folded the memo, slipped it into a fresh folder from the drawer, and tucked it into her tote bag like a bomb that hadn't exploded yet.

She was halfway through re-locking the drawer when something clattered loudly in the main room.

She froze.

Not dramatic thriller-froze. Just the quiet, measured stillness of someone who had grown up in a town where creaks and clatters often meant raccoons, drafty windows, or on very rare occasions, ghosts who wanted to correct your grammar.

She stood and crept into the hallway.

A display pedestal had tipped over.

Atop it, or rather beside it now, lay a brass plaque that had once identified Ashmere's founding family. The screw that held it in place had given way.

Or been loosened.

Isla stared at it.

Then muttered, "Of course."

She bent to pick it up, replaced it on the stand, then whispered, "If this is that raccoon again, I swear to God, I will register him to vote just to spite him."

No answer.

She exhaled, slow.

Still holding the key, now returned to her jacket pocket, she made her way to the front door, locking it behind her with the same care she'd use for a diary entry or a confession.

Because now, there was no more wondering.

No more fragments.

Meryl had found the reason to be afraid.

And Isla had just inherited it.

Chapter 20:Maps & Shadows

Isla on a hunch and perhaps hope, went back to the General Store to talk to Amos again.

Amos was behind the counter, carefully refilling a tin of licorice twists like it was a sacred ritual. He looked up with his usual grumble of a greeting, but it softened into something warmer when he saw her.

"Back again?" he asked. "You're going to wear out your welcome."

"You'd miss me," Isla said. "And I come bearing a question."

He raised an eyebrow.

"Do you have anything else?" she asked. "Maps, papers, anything Meryl might not have seen. Maybe tucked away in one of your apocalypse boxes?"

He gave a long sigh. "There's a box I didn't show her. Not because I was hiding it. I just… didn't think it mattered. Odds and ends. Water-damaged, mostly."

"Mind if I take a look?"

He disappeared into the back room without answering.

Isla leaned on the counter, eyeing a display of potato peelers shaped like ducks. She wasn't sure if it was whimsy or a crime against design.

Amos returned with a dust-covered plastic tub that looked like it had lost a fight with time twice.

"This is it," he said, placing it heavily on the counter. "If you find treasure, I expect naming rights."

She popped the lid.

Inside: a chaotic archive of rolled-up maps, yellowed paper, council drafts, flyers from forgotten town meetings, and a single expired coupon for a free turkey at Bayler's Groceries (1987).

She began sorting, Amos watching silently. He didn't hover. Just refilled a gum rack or more appropriately emptied it and placed the gum back in.

Ten minutes in, Isla unrolled a brittle parcel of parchment-like paper. Faded ink. Hand-drawn boundary lines.

"Wait a second," she murmured.

Amos wandered over, squinting. "Old town lot map. Might pre-date the '60s rebuild."

Isla traced her finger along the river's edge, then down toward the southern stretch of what was now Ashmere's community reserve.

"This" she tapped, "this whole area used to be part of the Croswell estate."

Amos whistled low. "That's a chunk of land."

"More than just the mansion. It extended down past the bend. But the current zoning plan doesn't include this section. It's been absorbed into public land."

She stared at the map, then folded it slowly.

"It's the kind of thing Clarissa wouldn't want to come to light," Isla said. "Not because she wants to develop the estate; but because part of it's already been taken. Quietly. Years ago."

Amos leaned on the counter, arms crossed. "Wouldn't be the first time this town swept something under the rug and called it legacy."

Before Isla could reply, the bell chimed again.

A couple entered, clearly tourists. Mid-forties, wearing matching vests and the kind of sun hats that suggested a recent devotion to hiking.

"Ooooh!" the woman said, zeroing in on a battered tin labeled *Yoyos – $2 each.*

Her husband picked one up reverently. "These are really old! Look! Bakelite rims."

Isla stepped back to let them marvel. Amos straightened with unexpected pride.

"We don't get many like those anymore," he said. "You wind 'em slow and flick with the wrist."

The couple ended up buying three. Amos gave them a little brown paper bag and even threw in a smile, which Isla hadn't known he offered with purchase.

When they left, she turned to him. "You soft-sell nostalgic toys better than you sell candy."

He sniffed. "Toys don't rot your teeth. And they come with memories."

Isla tucked the map gently into her bag.

"Thanks, Amos. You might've just given me the last piece."

He nodded, eyes thoughtful. "Just be careful. People start pulling threads like this, sometimes the whole town unravels."

She stepped outside into late afternoon sun, the kind that made everything look too gentle to hold secrets.

A voice called from a few steps away. "Hey there, Miss Winters."

She turned to find Deputy Ronny Patch, standing awkwardly near the bench by the postbox. He looked like he'd been rehearsing how to say hello for ten minutes and still wasn't sure it was the right move.

"Deputy," Isla said. "Are you stalking me?"

His face flushed immediately. "What? No. Good grief, I'd never, I mean, I was just, this is my patrol zone and"

"I'm joking, Ronny."

"Oh." He paused. "Right."

Isla smiled, just a little. "Relax. I appreciate the law keeping an eye out."

Ronny adjusted his belt like it might help him regain composure. "Well, uh… just let us know if you need anything. Officially."

"Will do."

He gave her a quick nod, then retreated toward the café with the urgency of a man who suddenly remembered he was meant to be somewhere else, or thought of pie.

Isla watched him go, then turned her face to the sun.

Just for a moment.

Then she walked on with one hand resting lightly on the map inside her bag.

The estate was bigger than anyone had claimed.

And the truth was getting harder to ignore.

It was nearly dark by the time Isla reached the edge of the Croswell property.

The fence had given up trying to stand straight years ago. It was slumped and rotting, with vines coiling like fingers over the faded sign that still existed:

CROSWELL – PRIVATE LAND – NO TRESPASSING

The wind picked up, tugging at a loose strip of tin nailed somewhere above the porch. It clanged rhythmically against the guttering, a hollow sound like a warning; or a distant memory.

Isla stepped over a broken plank and followed a faint trail through the long grass. Someone had been here recently. Maybe often.

The Croswell house was exactly as people remembered it, and nothing like the stories: two stories tall, peeling paint, porch sunken at one end. The windows were boarded over; all but one on the side, where the boards now lay in a loose pile at the base of the wall, as if someone had taken them off carefully... and not that long ago.

She circled toward it, boots soft on the moss. The sky behind her had turned bruise-purple. Somewhere in the distance, a bird called once and then stopped.

The rest of the forest had already gone quiet.

She crouched, pulled herself through the open window with a grunt that probably wasn't elegant, and dropped inside.

Inside, the air was still and heavy, like it had given up on being breathed.

She stood in what must have once been a hallway. Plaster peeled in thin ribbons from the ceiling, and dust clung to the walls like guilt. A sheet draped over something large in the corner. She lifted it and found a broken rocking horse, one side splintered, the smile on its painted face cracked in two.

"Comforting," she murmured.

A set of portraits hung askew on the far wall. Age had not been kind. One frame was empty, the photo inside long fallen. Another remained, but the figure's face had blurred with water damage, the eyes smudged into empty sockets, the mouth lost entirely. She stared at it too long.

She moved on.

A desk sat just inside what might have once been a sitting room. Crooked legs, chipped paint, and still on top a guestbook.

She hesitated, then flipped it open. Dust jumped up in protest.

Most of the entries were from decades ago. A dinner guest. A local councilor. A few signatures she couldn't make out. But near the bottom of the last page, written in a firmer, darker ink:

July 2 The lawyer is late again. I told Miranda this won't hold forever.

Isla's breath caught.

Miranda?

She flipped the page.

Nothing.

The rest was blank.

She closed the book gently, her fingers lingering on the edge of the desk.

A faint smell drifted in through the broken window; it was sour, chemical, like burned plastic or old varnish. Not woodsmoke. Not natural. And definitely not old.

She froze.

It was quiet again, too quiet.

The night had gone still. No crickets. No frogs.

She turned toward the window and saw movement.

A figure.

At the edge of the property, just past the willow trees near the riverbank. Standing still. Facing her direction.

They were too far away to make out, but the overcoat was unmistakable. Long, heavy, and out of place for the season. Even in Ashmere.

They didn't move.

Isla held her breath.

The figure finally turned, slow and deliberate, and walked into the trees. Not hurried. Not afraid.

As if they'd come to watch something and now, were done.

Isla backed away from the window. Slowly. Every nerve pulled tight like piano wire.

She waited five full minutes before she moved again.

Then she climbed back out the window and slipped through the overgrown trail in silence.

Behind her, the Croswell house didn't creak or groan or settle.

It just waited for a mystery to be solved.

Chapter 21: Letters

The museum didn't creak when Isla pushed the door open this time.

It sighed.

The kind of sigh you heard from old buildings when they were tired of pretending to be important. Or maybe just needed some tlc.

She stepped inside, pulling her jacket tighter against the early chill. Morning sun had barely climbed past the trees, casting light across the wooden floorboards in long, tired stripes. The air still held its new mix of burnt ash and cleaning products; what she now considered Ashmere's signature scent of intrigue.

No one was there. Again. But she didn't expect anyone to be.

She walked past the sign-in sheet, glanced at the latest entry. It was a delivery driver, and continued on to Meryl's office.

The crooked "Staff Only Please Knock (but gently)" sign still clung to the door by a single pin. It tilted further now, like even it had given up on rules.

Inside, the room remained as she remembered: intentionally cluttered, layered with the quiet chaos of someone who catalogued memories for a living.

But today, Isla wasn't after the obvious.

Something caught her eye. She dropped to her knees beside the far wall, where the wooden baseboard panel looked newer than the others, a touch less dusty, slightly warped. The kind of detail most people would miss.

She pried gently at the edge, her fingernails slipping, then grabbed a nearby ruler from the desk drawer and wedged it into the crack.

With a reluctant creak, the board popped free.

Behind it was a hollow cavity, maybe a foot deep. Inside: a few crumpled receipts, a broken stapler, and behind those items as if they were the camouflage: one stiff, yellowed envelope, sealed but unposted.

To: Office of Historical Property Claims
RE: Ashmere / Croswell Inheritance Query – URGENT

Isla sat back on her heels and carefully opened it.

The letter was typewritten, the kind with uneven ink pressure. Meryl must've dragged out the old typewriter from the archives. Every sentence was precise, deliberate. No wasted words.

165

To Whom It May Concern,

I am writing to formally request a review of historical ownership regarding the Croswell Estate land. Recent informal records in Ashmere's council files appear to show zoning changes and public usage approvals that do not align with the original estate trust conditions outlined in the 1928 deed.

I suspect, though cannot yet prove, that portions of the estate have been absorbed improperly by the township.

Please find attached:
• Summary of conflicting land maps (1952–1989)
• Extract from Ashmere Historical Society Museum records
• Annotated zoning proposal (unsigned copy)

I request legal and historical guidance on whether a claim may be pursued for improper land use or misappropriation of inherited trust assets.

I believe this matter may involve individuals currently serving on the town council, including former subcommittee members.

Please respond urgently. I am concerned that this issue, if not documented soon, may be deliberately erased.

Sincerely,
Meryl Hartley Ashmere Historical Society

Isla exhaled slowly. Then muttered, "This woman made bullet points. That's how you know she was serious."

She looked at the date. Just six weeks ago.

Meryl never mailed it.

Had she been waiting for more evidence? Scared to send it? Isla's stomach turned; had she already known someone would try to stop her?

She took a photo with her phone, then carefully slid the letter back into the envelope and tucked it into her bag. The kind of letter that didn't belong in a museum exhibit; but if Isla's hunch was correct maybe one day it would.

Behind her, a soft clank startled her.

She turned to find Mason Wilder, crouched by the front window frame, screwdriver in hand, balancing a loose pane of glass.

"You know," he said without looking up, "breaking and entering loses its charm when it becomes a habit."

"Wasn't breaking," Isla said. "The door sighed at me. Very welcoming."

Mason gave her a sidelong glance. "You're lucky no one called it in. Someone thought they saw movement."

"Was it you?"

"Maybe."

She tilted her head. "Stalking or civic duty?"

"Bit of both." He grinned. "Nancy Drew returns."

Isla rolled her eyes, but her lips curved. "If I'm Nancy Drew, does that make you the vaguely helpful male love interest with a suspiciously perfect jawline?"

"Only if I get to show up conveniently when the flashlight batteries die."

He returned to the window, tightening a screw. The silence was comfortable for a moment.

Then he asked, more gently, "You alright, Isla?"

She hesitated. "I found something. Meryl was planning to go public. She had evidence. Real stuff. But she didn't send it."

Mason paused. "Do you think she was stopped?"

"I don't know," Isla said. "But I think she was scared."

He stood, brushing dust off his hands. "You want help?"

"I think that's the first time anyone's asked me that in weeks."

"Well," he said, heading for the door, "doesn't mean I'm offering. Just curious."

She smirked. "Coward."

He winked and left.

Isla turned back to the office.

The envelope felt heavier in her bag than paper ought to.

She didn't know what it all meant yet but Meryl hadn't died confused. She'd died knowing.

And someone else knew that, too.

Chapter 22: Division

Ashmere had always been polite.

Even when it gossiped.

Even when it judged.

But today, Isla felt the air shift. Not icy, just cooler. Polished smiles held for half a second too long. Greetings that used to come with warmth now arrived with just enough distance to notice.

She pushed open the diner door. No one looked up, which was unusual. That was usually an Ashmere pastime.

The girl at the counter, Marla? Mia? used to scribble little smiley faces on receipts. Today, she didn't make eye contact.

Isla leaned in. "Large black, no sugar, please."

The girl nodded and turned. A minute later, she returned with a to-go cup and slid it across.

"There you go. On the house."

Isla blinked. "Oh. Thanks."

She took a sip. Then frowned. Then stared at the cup like it had betrayed her.

"This isn't coffee," she said flatly.

"No, it's chamomile," the girl replied, not unkindly. "Thought you looked like you could use something... calming."

Isla tilted her head, lips twitching. "Am I being tranquilized?"

The girl looked momentarily panicked. "No! I mean I just thought. Sorry. I can remake it."

Isla waved it off with a dry smile. "Don't worry. It's probably good for my aura."

She stepped aside, letting the next customer shuffle up, and carried the tea out like it might bite her.

On the bench outside, she sipped again. To Isla it was bitter and floral. She watched as two older women walked past, pausing mid-chat to glance at her. One of them murmured something. The other gave a half-smile, the kind that pretended to be kind and failed spectacularly.

Great. She was the town curiosity now.

She dumped the tea into the nearby planter and headed for the florist.

Tessa's shop still smelled like lavender and soil, same as always. A string of fairy lights blinked above the counter, and an old radio murmured soft lo-fi in the background.

Tessa was arranging a bouquet of dahlias when Isla entered.

"Oh, hey," Tessa said, startled but trying to smooth it out. "Didn't hear you come in."

"I walk like a ghost," Isla said. "New skill."

Tessa smiled weakly. "Right. Um, everything okay?"

Isla leaned on the counter, watching the flowers. "Have you noticed the town feels... off?"

Tessa hesitated. "People are just... adjusting."

"To what?"

"You. Asking questions. Stirring things." Tessa's hands moved faster, tucking stems. "Not everyone likes when things are stirred."

"They prefer them buried?"

Tessa didn't answer. The silence was awkward enough to be loud.

"You think I should stop?" Isla asked quietly.

Tessa looked up. Her eyes softened, but her voice stayed firm. "I think… maybe just take a breath. You always were curious. Remember when you took the teachers textbook as you were convinced the answers she was giving were lies."

Isla laughed. "I was eight. I needed answers."

Tessa added, "This isn't a story, Isla. It's the whole town. People live here. They don't want to be pulled into whatever this is becoming."

Isla nodded. "Got it. Just one thing, though."

"What?"

"If Meryl was killed over this, or if her death wasn't an accident… is everyone still okay with silence?"

Tessa looked like she wanted to say something. Instead, she turned back to the bouquet and whispered, "I need to finish this before the delivery."

Isla left quietly.

Outside, a new notice had been pinned to the town square board:
Council Session – Proposed Redevelopment Vote – Public Welcome
Below it: three bullet points outlining zoning discussions, infrastructure grants, and *"heritage site potential realignments."*

She stared at the bold text for a long moment.

Then reached for her phone and took a photo.

So that no matter how this ended, someone would remember the timing.

The sun had dipped below the hills by the time Isla turned the corner to her cottage.

The street was still. Just the hush of evening birds and the rustle of wind in the birches. She fumbled for her keys, halfway distracted by a text she hadn't answered, when her boot nudged something against the front step.

A folded piece of paper.

She bent to pick it up.

The text read: *Ashmere's not yours to fix.*

No signature. Blocky, careful handwriting. No smudges, no creases. Like it had been placed, not dropped.

She stood there, frozen in the blue half-light.

Then slowly unlocked the door and stepped inside.

The cottage looked exactly as she'd left it.

Mostly.

Her side drawer, the one by the couch, was cracked open. Just slightly.

The drawer with her photos, her phone charger, a stray journal, and the folder she'd labeled *"Maybe important, maybe not"* like a liar.

She crouched and opened it fully. Nothing missing. But the papers weren't in the right order. The journal had a page folded back. The charger cord was now looped too neatly.

Someone had been here.

Someone had time.

She checked the bedroom. No mess. No prints. Nothing out of place except the quiet itself.

She returned to the living room, sat down on the couch, and stared at the note in her hand.

Whoever wrote it hadn't come for violence. That would've been louder. Cruder. This was precision. This was a message.

She considered calling Mason. For backup. For logic. Maybe even just for comfort.

But he'd been helping fix broken plumbing at the school all week. He was stretched thin. And what could he do? Run prints off a Post-it? Knock on every door with a smirk and hope someone confessed?

She folded the note and slid it into her notebook instead.

No sense in reacting. Yet.

That night, she locked the door. Then the windows.

Then checked them again.

The kettle squealed like it knew she needed something. Isla was half convinced to interrogate it too.

She poured herself a cup of coffee, whilst having ptsd flashbacks to the Chamomile. She sat on the edge of her bed, and whispered to herself, "I should get a dog."

She looked around the cottage: one bedroom, one stubborn sofa, two and a half working lamps and a few old cupboards and tables.

"Yeah. Or a moat."

She left the light on by the front door. Not for comfort. Just to see if anyone walked past again.

And then she went to sleep. Sort of.

Chapter 23: Records and Groceries

The basement of the town hall smelled like wet paper and ambition gone to rot.

Isla descended the narrow staircase slowly, each wooden step groaning under the weight of history. Or maybe just poor maintenance. At the bottom, she fumbled for the chain-pull light. It clicked twice before the bulb flared to life with the sickly hue of old fluorescents.

A maze of filing cabinets, loose crates, and mildew-stained banker boxes filled the room. The kind of archive that had once been someone's pride and now survived on inertia and benign neglect.

She stepped carefully between stacks labeled with everything from *ASHMERE FLOOD RELIEF 1983* to *YOUTH SOCCER PERMITS (1991–1999)*.

In her jacket pocket, Mason's borrowed key ring clinked against itself; a small sound, oddly reassuring. He'd handed them over that morning with a shrug and a warning: "If anything bites, don't blame me."

She hadn't told him about the break-in. Or the note. Not yet.

She found a gray metal filing cabinet labeled *DEEDS /
TITLE TRANSFERS / ZONING – ARCHIVE*. The
drawers resisted like they hadn't been opened since the
Reagan administration. When one finally gave way, it
exhaled a puff of paper dust like a sigh from the past.

Most of the folders were warped from water damage,
likely flood runoff from a decade ago. But a handful
were legible. She skimmed past council zoning plans,
blank claim forms, until:

*Title Absorption Proposal – 1987 (Temporary Infrastructure
Allocation – Croswell Sector)*

Her eyes caught on a name halfway down the document:

Signed: Franklin Voss
Ashmere Infrastructure Review Committee Chair

Miranda's father.

Of course.

The notes were sparse but damning. A "temporary"
reallocation of land rights to allow for "public utility
access," with a vague clause stating "future review
contingent on claim activity."

There was no claim activity.

Not if the rightful heir was never told.

And if Meryl had only found this… thirty years too late.

Isla sat back on her heels, the folder open in her lap, the
edges slick with damp. The ink on one page had bled in
places, as if even the truth had tried to erase itself.

She flipped through the supporting notes; handwritten meeting minutes on thin yellowing paper. They discussed road access, flood planning, "low-impact temporary development" nothing permanent, nothing final.

But everything built since then had been quietly declared permanent by practice.

Miranda hadn't just stumbled into this. She'd grown up inside it.

Isla rubbed her temple. "What every girl dreams of. Moldy bureaucracy and generational guilt."

She slipped the document into a sleeve from her folder, careful not to smear the fading text, and zipped it into her bag.

Then she stood slowly and shut the drawer, leaving the past to creak shut behind her.

At the top of the stairs, she paused.

Somewhere above, the wind rattled a loose gutter. The town hall had settled back into its usual silence.

But for Isla, something louder had clicked into place.

Miranda Voss wasn't covering for herself.

She was continuing a cover-up she'd inherited.

The invitation arrived in an envelope with her name typed neatly, impersonally slid under her door.

Inside, a crisp cream card:

Miranda Voss
Welcomes you to Elmwood House
Tuesday, 11:00 a.m.
To discuss a matter of mutual interest

No RSVP. No option.

Just expectation.

Elmwood House was everything Isla's cottage wasn't.

Polished. Sculpted. Curated to within an inch of its sterile perfection.

The driveway curved with unnatural precision, lined with ornamental shrubs that probably had Latin names and personal stylists. The porch gleamed, the knocker untouched. Because obviously, no one *knocked* at Elmwood. They were buzzed in, or not at all.

Miranda answered the door herself. Her blouse was the kind of white that only existed in dry cleaner commercials, and her smile carried a faint shimmer of social sunscreen.

"Isla. Thank you for coming."

"I wasn't sure it was optional."

Miranda laughed, one note too long. "Come in."

The house felt too clean to feel lived in.

The living room looked like a magazine spread with all the warmth edited out. Cream walls, pale grey accents, not a single object out of place.

Miranda gestured toward a minimalist armchair.

"Tea? Coffee?"

"Got anything stronger?"

A pause.

"Kidding," Isla added, sitting down. "Mostly."

Miranda took the opposite seat; legs crossed with precision. "I'll be direct."

"Please do. We've had enough poetry."

"I've been watching your... involvement around town. Asking questions. Visiting places."

Isla folded her arms. "Yes, we have talked about this. Ashmere's a nice place to walk."

Miranda's smile didn't shift. "And dig."

She stood and crossed to a sideboard. Isla's eyes flicked to the wine rack beside it. Twelve bottles, arranged like a design feature rather than for drinking.

"Let me guess," Isla said. "Each bottle has a mood board and a portfolio."

Miranda chuckled lightly. Isla was convinced she did not get the joke.

She poured a glass of lemon water instead. "Isla, you strike me as someone who's... underutilized."

180

"That's one way to say unemployed."

"Another way," Miranda continued, "is *available*."

She returned, placing a folder on the coffee table between them.

"The council is forming a new Heritage Engagement Fund. A role will be created to lead public education about Ashmere's history. Stories, lectures, community outreach. I've had your name suggested."

Isla didn't touch the folder. "How generous."

"It's real," Miranda said. "Stipend included. Office space. Autonomy."

"And the catch?"

"No catch," Miranda said smoothly. "But of course, if you're working *with* the town, it would be wise to… avoid stirring unnecessary tension. The last thing we want is more grief."

"Of course."

Miranda sipped her water. "You're clever, Isla. That's rare here. Don't waste it shadowboxing ghosts."

Isla leaned forward, hands clasped.

"I think Meryl was trying to stop something. And I think someone stopped her first."

Miranda's smile tightened. "That's an unkind suggestion."

"So is murder."

They held each other's gaze for a long moment.

Then Isla stood.

"Thanks for the offer," she said. "But I'm more of a freelance meddler."

Miranda rose too, smoothing her skirt. "Think about it."

"I did."

She left without shaking hands.

Outside, the sun cut through the cloud cover like someone had remembered to turn the lights back on.

Isla walked faster than usual, her breath sharp. Eager to leave the premise.

That hadn't been a conversation.

That had been containment, dressed up in courtesy and lemon water.

The general store was becoming like a second home for Isla. She felt grounded in its timeless space. Amos was halfway through restocking the fridge with peach soda, muttering at it like it owed him money.

Isla wandered in without much of a plan. She didn't need groceries. Just something to reassure her. Something normal.

She'd barely stepped past the register when a voice chirped near the spice rack.

"Excuse me, dear?"

Mrs. Penelope Hark, small and birdlike in a lavender coat, was holding a packet of dill and watching Isla with curious eyes.

"I wonder if we might speak. Outside."

They stood on the wooden stoop as the breeze tugged at the hanging "CLOSED" sign. Isla was convinced Amos changed his sign to closed regularly just to try to deter actual customers.

Mrs. Hark kept her voice low. "I didn't want to say anything earlier. I wasn't sure it mattered. But now…"

Isla leaned in slightly. "Go on."

"I saw Miranda Voss. Two nights before the festival. By the river. With Meryl."

That alone made Isla's heart pause.

"They were talking," the older woman continued, "or arguing, I couldn't quite tell. It looked tense. Miranda was gesturing. Meryl stood her ground. But I wasn't close enough to hear a word. I didn't want to interrupt."

"Did they leave together?"

"No. Miranda walked off first, quick-like. Meryl stayed behind a while." She shook her head. "But Meryl was *alive* after that. We all saw her again at the festival. I too remember seeing her, laughing with someone near the jam stall."

So, whatever happened hadn't happened yet.

"Maybe it was nothing," Mrs. Hark added, tone uncertain. "Old friends falling out. Or something personal."

"Maybe," Isla said, though her gut tightened.

"But I thought… well, if you're asking questions, that might matter."

"It might."

Mrs. Hark hesitated. "Just… be careful, dear. The Voss family has deep roots here. They don't like being tugged."

"I'm getting that sense."

Back inside, Amos was watching her from behind the counter, a skeptical brow raised.

"That looked serious."

Isla grabbed a licorice bar off the stand. "Not everything has to be romantic, Amos."

"Didn't say it was."

She smirked, dropped a coin on the counter, and headed for the door.

Outside, the wind had picked up. Leaves skittered across the pavement like whispers trying to catch up.

Isla tucked the memory away like a matchstick.

It wasn't fire yet.

But maybe, just maybe it was smoke.

Isla tried to thread it all together.

Meryl had clearly been digging into the Croswell estate; pulling on old threads, chasing records that hinted at something just out of reach. Clarissa and Miranda were both tied to her... and to the property. Different ties, but knots all the same.

Then there was Hank, spotted arguing with Meryl not long before her death, and later seen with charcoal-stained hands after the museum fire. Maybe nothing. Maybe not.

And that shadowed figure near the estate. The one who slipped away too quickly. Was it one of them? Or someone else entirely?

The facts didn't line up cleanly yet. But Isla wasn't struggling with the *who* so much as the *how*.

None of them looked like a murderer.

Then again, what does a murderer look like, really? She thought.

Chapter 24: Storms

The rain came down like it had a grudge.

First as a whisper, then as a slap.

Isla stood at her window and watched Ashmere disappear under sheets of grey, the trees outside bowing like they knew better than to fight it. Powerlines swayed, the porch light flickered once, and somewhere off toward the river, thunder rolled long and low, like an angry spirit streaming through the skies.

Inside, the cottage felt too small for the storm.

She'd spread her notes across the kitchen table. A collection of photos, scribbled timelines, a rough map of Croswell property boundaries, all weighted down with whatever was within reach: a jar of pens, a candle, half a grapefruit.

The kind of chaos that looked accidental but wasn't.

She stared at the same line of scribbled names for the fourth time. Meryl. Miranda. Clarissa. Hank. She'd circled the word *inheritance* twice and then crossed it out.

The power blinked.

Just a hiccup: off, then on again. But enough to send the kettle into a quiet panic and reset the digital clock on the stove to 12:00.

Isla stilled.

Then the lights cut out entirely.

Silence. Heavy, waiting.

She sighed and reached for her phone, using its torch to cast a lopsided glow over the room. "Of course."

The wind kicked up outside. Something metal clanged followed by what might've been a branch cracking against the back fence.

Or not a branch.

She got up and checked the locks on the front and back doors. They held. But she double-checked the windows just in case. The storm made everything feel thinner. It was as if the walls weren't walls, just suggestions that could be removed at any time.

In the living room, the shadows moved like old memories.

She considered dragging a chair in front of the door. Or the laundry basket.

Instead, she stood there, arms crossed, muttering, "That thing can't even hold socks. Who am I kidding?"

Another crack of thunder shook the glass. The cottage lights surged briefly back to life… then failed again. She gave up and lit the candle with a match that took two tries.

The soft glow spilled across the table, catching a glint on the photo she'd printed of the zoning plan. Clarissa's name. Half-scanned. Half-hiding.

She sat down.

The rain battered harder, a relentless drumbeat against the roof. Her head throbbed to match.

She hadn't slept properly in days. Not since the note. Not since the shadow in the woods. Not since Meryl started speaking from the spaces between things.

She didn't believe in ghosts.

But she believed in things unfinished.

A sharp *tap* against the window jolted her upright. Not hard. Just a single *tap*, deliberate, like a finger knocking once.

She turned the torch back on and crept toward the window. Nothing.

Just the storm. The dark. The glass fogged from her breath.

Still, she stood there longer than necessary, heart ticking like it had a deadline.

When she finally sat back down, the candle was nearly half gone.

She leaned her head on her arms, staring at the flicker.

Maybe she was too far in now. Maybe that was the point.

People didn't warn you unless you were close to something worth hiding.

Outside, the thunder rolled again; not distant now, but right over Ashmere, shaking the bones of the town.

And this time, Isla didn't flinch.

Chapter 25: Confrontation

Miranda Voss's real estate office was exactly what Isla expected.

Glass walls, cream carpet, brushed metal nameplate on the desk. A few generic landscape prints hung on the walls. Lake scenes, sunlit forests, the kind of beauty that didn't mean anything and had been chosen from a catalogue. The front desk assistant barely glanced up when Isla walked in, her name already typed into the schedule.

"Ms. Voss is expecting you," the woman said, as if Isla were here for a mortgage consultation, not an unraveling.

Miranda's office was at the end of the hall. The blinds were half drawn, softening the light but not the mood. Isla was glad to be meeting Miranda somewhere relatively public.

Miranda stood behind her desk, framed by neat shelves and a single orchid in bloom. She wore slate gray, hair pinned. Control incarnate.

"I assume you're not here about buying," she said.

"Not unless you've got riverfront truth going cheap," Isla replied.

Miranda gestured to the chair. "Sit, if you'd like."

Isla didn't.

She pulled a folded sheet from her coat pocket and laid it on the desk. The development plan, the one with Clarissa Finch's signature, with penciled zoning notes, with proposed sales that shouldn't exist.

Miranda didn't touch it.

"You know what that is," Isla said.

"I know what it looks like."

"It looks like Clarissa planned to force the Croswell estate to auction. And you were going to buy it."

Silence.

"Then sell it back to the council," Isla continued. "At a tidy markup, no doubt."

Miranda's hands folded lightly at her waist. No twitch. No denial. But her stillness was louder than a confession.

"Clarissa had the idea," she said, voice low. "She said it would help the town. That if we moved quickly, no one would question it."

"She didn't mention Meryl?"

Miranda's jaw flexed. "She underestimated her. We both did."

"She found the deed."

"Yes. And she made it very clear she planned to stop the sale."

"So, you went to talk to her."

Miranda's eyes finally moved. Down. Then back to Isla.

"It wasn't meant to happen like that," she said. "Clarissa had the idea. I was just trying to talk to her. That's all it was. But she wouldn't let it go."

Isla waited.

"She was emotional. So was I. We were by the river. I pushed her. Not hard, but.." Miranda's voice cracked slightly, then reset. "Just… just enough. She slipped. Hit her head. Fell in."

"You left her there."

"I didn't know what else to do."

"You dressed her. Staged it."

"I panicked," Miranda said quietly. "I lost one of her gloves. I couldn't find it. I thought if it looked accidental…"

She trailed off. Not with drama. Just exhaustion.

Isla stepped closer to the desk, voice steady. "You burned documents. Broke into my cottage. Left a note."

Miranda didn't deny it.

"I was trying to keep this contained," she said. "It wasn't just about me. The town… the deal… it was supposed to help everyone."

"By taking something that wasn't yours," Isla said. "And silencing the one person who stood in your way."

There was a long pause.

"You don't understand Ashmere," Miranda said finally. "This place runs on balance. On quiet deals and things that are out of sight. Meryl forgot that. You never learned it."

"Maybe it's time Ashmere forgot how to forget," Isla said.

She picked up the document from the desk and turned to leave.

At the door, she hesitated.

"You asked me to stop asking questions. Maybe you should've asked yourself why I started."

Miranda didn't speak again.

But as Isla stepped past the quiet receptionist and those frozen, cheerful home listings, she realized something: Miranda had built a life on appearances. And Isla had just cracked the glass.

The file felt heavier than paper had any right to be.

Isla sat on the bench outside Ashmere's police station, the Croswell documents tucked inside a manila folder on her lap. Across the street, the general store was closing early, and the sky was doing that slow pastel fade that only small towns noticed.

She'd written a cover note. Short. Simple. Just the facts.

She hadn't signed it.

Inside, she could see Deputy Ronny Patch behind the front desk, shifting papers. He wasn't the best cop. Or the worst. But he was consistent. And right now, consistency felt like a lifeline.

She thought about Meryl; her notes, her neatly labeled folders, the key taped under the drawer like a breadcrumb trail for someone who might care enough to follow.

She thought about Miranda. All that polish and control, undone not by rage, but by panic. By the moment someone fights too hard to protect something they were never meant to hold.

And Clarissa. Already gone. Her ambition extinguished not by justice, but timing.

Ashmere wasn't a town full of villains.

It was a town full of stories. And secrets. And people who thought they were doing what needed to be done.

Isla exhaled slowly.

Then stood.

She walked inside and handed the folder to Ronny without a word. He looked confused for a moment, then flipped it open. His brow furrowed deeper with each page. When he looked up, there was a question already forming.

Isla cut it off gently.

"I don't want thanks. I don't want involvement. Just... do what you think is right."

He nodded. Not quickly. Not confidently. But he nodded.

She left the station before he could say anything else.

The next morning, she stopped by the general store for tea bags and a second opinion on the weather.

Amos was restocking batteries by the front counter. "Storm missed us," he said, without being asked.

Isla offered a half-smile. "Good. I've had enough drama this week."

She was just about to head out when the sound of tires on gravel turned her head.

The town cruiser pulled up out front of the station. Ronny got out, opened the back door.

Miranda Voss stepped out slowly of the building, flanked by another officer but not forced. Her blazer was buttoned, her chin up.

Isla watched through the dusty window. She didn't move. Didn't speak.

But she saw Miranda look over once. She was not looking at her, but at the street. At Ashmere.

Then the car door closed, and the cruiser pulled away.

Chapter 26: Another Festival

The river shimmered under the late afternoon sun, golden and lazy like it had nothing left to prove. Tents flapped gently along the bank, and the scent of kettle corn and grilled sausage carried across the water like a memory trying to sweeten itself.

Ashmere's Autumn Festival was back.

Smaller this time. Quieter.

There were fewer vendors, fewer crowds, but still music, still color. Still the illusion and sometimes the reality, that life went on.

Isla stood near the cider booth, a paper cup in her hand and a scarf tucked against the wind. It was the kind of day that made you believe the past could be softened even if just a little.

"Looks better than last festival," said a familiar voice beside her.

Mason Wilder, hands in pockets, relaxed for once.

"Fewer people, but it's a new season," Isla replied.

He smirked. "I heard about what happened. Not all the details, but… enough."

"Me too," Isla said.

They stood in companionable silence for a few moments.

"Guess you're not going anywhere," Mason said, not a question.

"I thought about it," she admitted. "But I've already done the hard part. Got the Binnie to respect me. Feels wasteful to leave now."

He chuckled. "Next time you move to a quiet town, read the fine print."

"I did," she said. "It was written in invisible ink."

Down near the river's edge, kids were tossing stones into the shallows. Someone started a guitar cover of an old folk song that Isla couldn't quite name but had heard a hundred times.

Then, as if summoned by narrative duty, Binnie materialized beside her.

"Did you hear?" she said, eyes gleaming like a local crow who had stumbled across something shiny. "Miranda's preliminary hearing's been delayed. Some talk of her legal team arguing diminished responsibility. But I bet the courtroom sketch artist will have a field day."

Isla blinked. "Hello, Binnie."

"Anyway, I think it's all terribly exciting. Did I tell you I once sat next to a juror on a flight to Chicago? Absolutely useless conversationalist, but the stories afterward.."

Isla let the words wash over her. It was nice, in a strange way, to hear something that didn't demand her reaction.

Eventually, Binnie trailed off, distracted by a new audience, and vanished just as suddenly.

The sun dropped lower.

Children were herded home. The cider tent closing.

Mason touched her shoulder lightly before heading off to help pack up.

Isla stayed behind a moment longer.

She looked out over the river, the light dappling across the surface like whispers.

Everything wasn't fixed.

But it was moving.

And maybe that was enough.

The river was quieter without the music.

Late evening had crept in, painting the world in deep blue shadows and threads of wind. Isla stood just past the festival grounds, where the grass grew longer and the path lost its ambition.

She held Meryl's photo, the one from the museum, the one without a label. Now she knew it was the Croswell estate. Now she knew why it mattered.

"I hope we did you some justice," she murmured, running a thumb along the edge.

It wasn't poetic. But it was real.

Ashmere had cracked, then settled. Not cleanly, but maybe honestly. Miranda would face consequences. The Croswell land dispute was now a legal headache with multiple claims and footnotes. But now it was visible. No longer buried under whispers and zoning shadows.

And Isla?

She was still in her dusty cottage.

Still nursing the occasional cup of coffee.

Still going to the general store for supplies and being handed new gossip like it was a receipt.

But something in her had shifted.

She didn't need to leave to feel in motion.

rustle outside the cottage window made her glance up from her tea.

At first, she thought it was the wind again, or maybe the old drainpipe rattling like it did when the temperature dropped.

But then she saw it, just beyond the porch steps, paws on the edge of the flowerbed, fur slightly damp from the evening air.

The raccoon.

Her raccoon.

It stared at her.

She stared back.

It didn't hiss this time. Didn't scramble or knock over the broom.

Just held her gaze for a moment too long, as if weighing something. Then the raccoon turned and padded slowly into the underbrush, tail swaying like a flag lowered in peace.

Isla let out a slow breath.

"Well," she said to no one in particular, "if that's not a resolution, I don't know what is."

She got up, tucked the photo back into the drawer with the rest of her notes, and turned off the porch light.

No music, no answers. Just peace. And a little space to breathe.

Thank you for visiting Ashmere. I hope you enjoyed getting to know Isla and her little river town. If you'd like to follow along for future mysteries (and raccoon encounters), you can find me at www.farbellum.com.